Finding Poppies

VICKI B. WILLIAMSON

Copyright © Vicki B Williamson 2016

All rights reserved.

ISBN-10: 0692633014
ISBN-13: 978-0692633014

DEDICATION

For my husband, Mark – for always believing.

For my brother, Brian – Are you dazzled?

CONTENTS

Chapter 1	7
Chapter 2	19
Chapter 3	26
Chapter 4	35
Chapter 5	43
Chapter 6	47
Chapter 7	53
Chapter 8	58
Chapter 9	64
Chapter 10	70
Chapter 11	72
Chapter 12	83
Chapter 13	89
Chapter 14	96
Chapter 15	104
Chapter 16	124
Chapter 17	134
Chapter 18	143
Chapter 19	153
Chapter 20	161
Chapter 21	173
Chapter 22	179
Epilogue	187

1

My name is Ellen Thompson and I have a story to tell.

As I look back now, having withstood the past few weeks, the good and the bad, I'm not sure if I believe it all happened — so I'll grant you a bit of skepticism. Before you stop me — before you hold up your hands and shake your head in disbelief — understand we can all be stronger and braver than we first imagine.

So strap in, hang on and let's go back...

2015

I stare down at the dead body and realize I'm panting. With a deep breath and then another, I attempt to quiet and slow my breathing. My skin has broken out in a cold sweat and I feel dizzy. It's absolutely silent in this house.

The next thing I know, I'm outside bent over, retching into the hot summer air.

This isn't the first dead body I've seen, but it's certainly the first murdered body; and the neat little hole in his forehead gives me all the evidence I need that this poor man has been murdered. I never thought this week would turn out like this. I never thought I would be here — in this predicament, today.

Two Days Ago...

Arriving home from work, I heave a sigh and stifle a yawn. Though I have my dream job and love to work with art, some days are taxing, both mentally and physically. To get where I am, I've worked long and hard, studying in college to the elimination of other things. I've always known exactly where I want to be and what I want to do with my life.

I love my job at the Detroit Institute of Art, where I work as an Associate Curator of European Art. European Art and its history have always called to me. My parents often told stories of how I was born to work with the great masters. Even as a child I loved to visit the museums. They were a fantasy world where my imagination could thrive. As young as five years of age I understood part of the magic of the museum was how the story and the fantasy changed with every turn of a corner. It might be Egypt, where the wind blew hot and arid over the dunes; Medieval Europe, where I could hear the shout and clang of swords on armor as men fought in the rain; or Africa, where the roar of the lions made me shiver with fear and excitement. Every hall led to another tale and every tale could be wherever or whenever my thoughts took me.

In the art-filled rooms I would stand transfixed and stare at the work of masters Monet, Van Gogh, da Vinci and many others. Even at such a tender and innocent age, the paintings spoke to me of their history and beauty.

My parents would visit quietly behind me; their whispers echoing off the ceiling as they discussed surprise and pride in my innate appreciation of something they loved so well. The memory of the museum visits filled me with a sense of warmth and peace, safety and acceptance.

As I grew to adulthood, the ritual of the museum visits would be practiced many times over until I was as at home with art and history as if I was in my own bedroom surrounded by my things. It was a love, nurtured in my parent's love, which would shape my life.

A sad smile creases the corner of my mouth at the thought of them and I reach up, unconsciously, to touch the chain and medallion I wear around my neck. It was a present from my parents and since their death from a car accident, I never take it off. I gently stroke the medallion. It's a circle about the size of a silver dollar that's bronze with a hole in the middle — like foreign money. I don't know what it is, or where they found it, but I love it. It's unique like them and like me too, I guess. Their absence is an ache that never ceases. It tears into my heart but I know they're proud of all I've accomplished and the person I've become.

Ah, Home Sweet Home. I love my apartment, my haven. With a smile I study my space. It's filled with many well-loved items: small things, old things, things treasured from my childhood and items I've purchased as an adult. Things such as an antique rag doll in a faded gingham dress. She's been well loved through the ages and now her face barely has features. I imagine a young girl kissing her so often their image was whipped off. Or my little tin milkman windup toy. He's not very large, but I was lucky to find him so well preserved. Looking at him, I see the industrious, earnest look on his face. All around me are items that fill me with contentment and make me feel welcome. As far back as I remember I've enjoyed finding a piece of art or history and pursuing it with dogged determination. I don't always come out the winner, but more often than not, it comes home with me.

My newest desire promises to be a beautiful 1920 art deco hand mirror, if the seller can be believed. For the past week we've discussed its purchase and worked out the fine details via the internet. We're close to coming to an agreement and I'm excited to lay my hands on it.

I come in my door, close and lock it and set my purse on the floor. Opening a few windows, I welcome the sounds of the city: cars honk, children play and dogs bark. I take a deep breath, enjoying the smells — heat, exhaust and a mixture of ethnic foods and let the peace of home sink into my bones. *Yep,* I think with a wry smile. *Ugly sofa is still here. Why can't the furniture fairies come and replace it with a beautiful, modern one?* As I fall backward onto the ugly but comfortable piece, I put my feet up and speak out loud, "Hello, little apartment. It's good to be home."

*****

The next morning I wake with a bright and sunny smile, excited and ready for my day. Quickly, I roll out of bed and jump into the shower. It's been a couple of weeks coming but today is the day. The mirror will be mine! I love to travel and really love to purchase personal treasures while I'm in a different country; but I have to admit, nothing compares to finding one close to home. Coming out of my bathroom, I do a little jig into my living room. The internet seller has finally come to an agreement on a price. Luckily, he lives in the same city as me. I'm to meet him later at his home in downtown Detroit - - *Ok, so it isn't the best of neighborhoods, but this mirror proves to be worth it.* I have no worries about the place of our meeting. I'm nothing if not confident. I've talked myself out of lots of situations.

When I step out of my car, however, I almost decide that confidence is overrated. The neighborhood has definitely seen better days. All the houses look vacant, with peeled paint and cracked foundations. Very few even have their windows intact. There's a faint smell of rotting garbage in the hot and heavy air. I dig into my purse for the seller information to double check the address.

As I read the paper, I nod and mutter. "Yep, McDougal Street, this is where he lives." I look from the paperwork to the street with a grimace. Sharply, I berating myself. "Quit being a baby, El!" *At least your little old car will be safe parked here, she fits right in. It's now or never!* With a sigh, I walk up the heaved and weeded sidewalk. The house, which had once been white, has faded to gray — at least what's left of the paint. It's an old two story and still has the structure to show it was once a beautiful house in a nice neighborhood. The front door hangs slightly ajar and one of the windows is cracked. The only sound is a cat screeching in the alley behind the house. Time stands still.

As I approach the door I catch a faded glimpse of my reflection. I'm an attractive, tall brunette woman, if I do say so myself — one my Great Aunt Mabel calls "big boned", bless her heart. I dressed casually in jeans and a t-shirt and threw on a navy blazer at the last minute. Shifting to knock on the door I swear I see movement inside, but don't know if this reassures me. There's no answer, so I knock again — harder.

"Hello? My name is Ellen Thompson. I have an appointment with Mr. Bell."

"Ah, hell," I mutter under my breath when no one answers the door. "Probably isn't even a mirror to sell. Nice wild goose chase."

I step back and turn away to pull my car keys from my purse when the door opens a crack. I shift back around — a little rat-like man peers at me from behind the door. He's short with gray greasy hair, crooked glasses and an odor that falls somewhere in between unwashed human and rotten potatoes, surprised I catch a whiff of flowers. His faded red and black-checked shirt has seen better days, with a week's supply of food dried on it. With a look of uncertainty, I take a step backward.

"Miss Thompson?" he asks. His voice is low and gravely and has an unused quality. I can detect an accent. I think he sounds Italian.

"Yes, I'm Ellen Thompson. Are you Mr. Bell?"

"Yes, yes. Please come in. Quickly now…" he steps back, gestures and opens the door just wide enough for me to squeeze through. As I move past him he looks up and down the street as though expecting trouble. My desire for the mirror is greater than my disquiet about this odd little man, so I step over the threshold and the door shuts behind me with a finality I hope I'm imagining.

The interior is as bad as the outside; worse, really, because any thought of a breeze is gone. It smells of the man, old food and possibly cat urine. Items are stacked over every surface - tables, couches; everything is covered with papers, old magazines, bags and an array of unidentifiable stuff with a deluge of dust. The curtains are open partially and dust motes move lazily in the stagnant air. The wallpaper is cracked and peeled — it looks like a three-day-old sunburn. The house and the man haven't been cleaned in ages and I repress the need to sneeze.

Lovely, I wrinkle my nose. *Well, in and out and this'll be a distant, unpleasant memory.* I cock my head and try to catch his eye. "Thank you for meeting with me, Mr. Bell. Do you have the mirror we spoke of?" Staying near the doorway, I keep the wall to my back. I'm not threatened by Mr. Bell and honestly, considering his size, I figure if push comes to shove I can take him. Still, no need to invite trouble. One thing I've learned from years in a major city — don't be dumb. Keep your eyes open and be prepared to defend yourself in any way you can. Be smart and stay out of bad situations. I hope this isn't a bad situation...

Mr. Bell fidgets. His hands are never calm and he's swaying, shifting his weight from foot to foot. In response, I unconsciously roll onto the balls of my feet, ready for action. He says, "Yes, Yes..." His eyes jump about, not staying too long on anything and they never make contact with mine. Mirror or not, my instincts scream at me and I decide to forfeit it and get out of the house when he turns to a bureau. My attention is momentarily caught by the old bureau — I can't help but admire it. With a little work and kindness it could be beautiful again. It's quite faded and has been treated cruelly in the past, but it is a lovely cherry wood. Mr. Bell pulls open the middle drawer and with a screech of metal on wood, he shifts the contents to lift a bundle. The cloth is old, dirty and discolored but my interest is captured and I want to see what it holds. I'm not going anywhere.

Mr. Bell brings the bundle to the table, lays it down carefully and steps back. I look at it, and then at him, waiting. Neither of us moves. I'm not entirely sure what he wants me to do and I don't want to rush him — he's barely holding it together. Not only do his eyes circle the room, but his lips quiver and there's a fine line of drool leaking down his chin and onto his shirt, where it adds to his general lack of appeal. As we stand there, he twitches and scratches the right side of his neck, leaving red marks that begin to ooze blood. I feel a mixture of sympathy for his plight and concern for my health when the cat screams again. He jerks and blinks — seems to come awake.

"There's the mirror," he says and indicates the bundle.

I pull the bundle apart with my fingertips. An old familiar tingling starts at the top of my head. I've had this feeling for as long as I can remember. It precedes important moments. Important discoveries. The cloth is soiled, stiff with age and stained with substances I don't want to know about. I have a fleeting thought — *I'm so glad I have my hand sanitizer.* As the wrap falls away...

The mirror isn't an authentic 1920 hand mirror, it can't possibly be that old. *Why the Buzz? What is it about this mirror? Why is it special?*

I'm concerned by the finish and the flower motif which is too perfect to be created by hand. It's a beautiful mirror, but disappointment weighs me down. I utter a sigh. "Um? Mr. Bell. Can you tell me how you came to own the mirror?" I ask with a tip of my head.

"My *La Sorella* had it."

I raise my eyebrows. He is Italian. "Your sister?" *Interesting, I wonder what the story behind that is.* "Well? I hate to tell you this, but I believe the mirror is a reproduction. It's not actually 100 years old."

"What do you mean? It's my *Sorella's*."

"Yes, Sir, I understand, and it is quite beautiful." I risk the survival of my sense of smell as I step closer and point at the mirror. "As you see when you look closely, all the swirls and markings are perfect like it was made by a machine. If it were the age we're thinking the silver, which is often plated over brass, would be marred in spots. The silver on this mirror is completely intact."

He seems, suddenly, to wake to what's happening and what I'm saying. Making eye contact and stepping forward, he looks even more confused. As he moves close his scent, like something out of a garbage bin, stops my breath. I tip my face into my hand and clear my throat. I don't want to offend him, so I breathe shallowly and try to be subtle as I move back a step. I wait to see if he will respond and to see what this might mean for the purchase of the mirror. I want it, as it's beautiful and I need to know why it causes my senses to buzz, but not for the price we originally negotiated.

"But you agreed! I must sell this mirror. You must buy it!" He's almost howling by the time he finishes.

With a knot of my brows, I put my hands up in a pacifying motion, quick to reassure him, "I'm still interested in purchasing this piece, Mr. Bell. As I said, it's very pretty. I just don't think it's worth the amount we agreed upon — perhaps we could renegotiate?"

A short time later I leave Mr. Bell's house with my new purchase safe in my bag. My mind is occupied with the mirror. I should have been more aware of my surroundings. I should have noticed the men down the street — should have seen them now and perhaps saved myself some heartache later...

MARCO

Outside, two men watch from their rental car as the woman leaves the house. They don't know what she's doing here but they do know their job just became more complicated.

"You see, Marco, I told you if we wait it would cause problems."

The other man doesn't even glance his way — he continues to watch the woman. He's a big man with dark brown hair and the face of a career fighter — scarred and hard.

The woman looks up and down the street as she nears an old silver car. She unlocks it, gets in and pulls away.

"Follow her," Marco says. They wait momentarily while she gets a lead on them before trailing.

When the woman parks at an apartment complex, the men watch her from a distance. She crosses the parking lot quickly: with a confident, long-legged stride. They enter the building a short distance behind her and catch sight of her as she goes into the stairwell, heading up. They give her time and follow only to hear the door on the fourth floor open and close. Quickly, they climb the stairs, open the door and observe her entering an apartment. As they glance at one another, they exchange a silent agreement. They'll be back and they'll find what she has. The Lady will want a full report.

JOE

Joe Bell feels relief like a weight off his chest when he realizes the mirror is no longer in his possession. For the first time in a long time, he can breathe naturally. The mirror, and its secrets, has been nothing but trouble for years. He will cut all ties with his past. No longer will he be at the beck and call of anyone. He's his own man and will make his own decisions. For four long years he's lived a life that is a lie, but no more. Soon he will speak with another complication — his partnership, an unwilling one on Joe's part. He will end that relationship as well and soon, soon he'll be able to start again, to have a real life. Perhaps he'll even return to Italy — the place of his birth. He inhales deeply, sighs and imagines he smells the crisp tanginess of the ocean and the earthiness of the vineyards. Yes, he will sever all of this business and start anew. With a troublesome thought, he squints his eyes. *The only continued connection with the past is hidden elsewhere. I should have given the woman the other items as well — make a clean break from all of it.* Joe knows how to contact her due to their conversations on the internet site; he'll tempt her with something else, another item to sell.

ELLEN

Arriving home I'm glad to walk through the door of my apartment. *Wow! What a weird day!* I lock my door, set down my purse and pull off my blazer to toss it over a chair. Needing something soothing, I turn the stereo on low, open the kitchen window and breathe deeply of the fresh air, relishing the feel of the breeze on my face. I pull the mirror from my bag and stand in the sunlight to look it over. *Yep. It was a good buy, and an adventure.* Mr. Bell let the mirror go for $50 which made us both happy. It's attractive and as I hold it in my hands the crown of my head vibrates. This vibration or The Buzz, as I've referred to it since I can remember, is not really a sound or a movement but somewhere in between. I used to think everyone felt this. Felt it when they looked for a lost item or if they thought hard, really hard, about something significant. Soon enough I realized I was different. Kids at school have a way of waking you up to that. I quit mentioning this sensation. Quit reaching for it. I didn't want to be different and I still don't. Different is overrated.

Enough nostalgia, I think and study the mirror in my hand.

Though not a true antique, I like it and it'll be a nice, usable accent on my dresser. It's quite ornate, the silver etched and swirled around the outside. I've always been tactile and my love of an object grows with my handling of it. As I clean the mirror it'll cement its place in my possessions. Wiping it down, I inspect it. Being this close to it for an extended time not only has my Buzz working but my hands are slightly numb. *What's with it?* The mirror seems to be just a mirror. Even with the Buzz, I'm calm. I love this type of activity. I have soothing piano music on and hum as I work. The sun shines and the mirror is truly beautiful. About a half hour in I realize I'm going to need smaller tools for all those swirls. *Ear Swabs! All-purpose ear swabs! And my magnifying glass. Staples of a girls cleaning kit.*

After a while, I squint my eyes and utter "What the...?" On the leading edge near the bottom the swab is caught on something. Is it broken? $50 and it's broken. *Just my luck*, I think with a shake of my head. Upon closer inspection, I realize smaller tools are needed for this finer work. In the bathroom I get my tweezers and plyers I keep for just this sort of thing. As I work closely on the piece that seems to be broken, something slides and clicks and the back of the mirror falls off in my lap. I jump a little and exclaim, "Oh! What? Well hell." I glance at the mirror back and then turn it over to study where it came from. My brow furrows and my eyes narrow when I see a folded piece of paper in the back of the mirror. "What...?"

Tentatively, I reach to touch the paper and it crinkles. The Buzz intensifies and I think, *Aha*. Grasping the edge, I pull the paper from the mirror. It's slightly discolored but of a good quality — fine stationary perhaps. I set the mirror down on the side table and place the back alongside the body of the mirror. I unfold the paper gently to see faded script written in a bold hand:

My dearest Maria,

I am eternally sorry for risking your safety in Cairo and I know you understand why I must leave you. We will never be safe while in possession of my sin. I'm sorry but I am unable to give up the Poppies! It calls to my soul in a way I am unable to understand or control. Remember our love and perhaps one day I will be free.

   Angelo

I reread the letter three times in an attempt to make sense of it. *Poppies? Cairo?* With a frown I stare at the paper. *What is this note? How did it get into the mirror and why?* I'm intrigued by this unforeseen development with my new mirror, and my memory is spiked by the mention of Cairo and Poppies. I set the note down on the table and go into my bedroom to dig in my closet. In the back I locate a box of articles and pull it forward. It's full of items I've kept that are of interest to me. Halfway through I find what I'm looking for.

Cairo Times

Van Gogh $55 Million 'Poppy Flowers' Theft in Cairo Blamed on Lax Security

The theft from a Cairo museum of a painting by Vincent van Gogh valued at $55 million took place when only seven out of 43 security cameras were functioning...

A chill runs down my spine. *Really? Could this be related to the note in my mirror?* I tap the article of paper on my knee and sit back on my haunches, thinking. I vaguely remember two Italians were questioned about the disappearance of the art work before they boarded a plane to Italy. They were two of only nine people to visit the Mohamed Mahmoud Khalil Museum in Cairo that day. *Could those two Italians have been Maria and Angelo? How did Mr. Bell come by this? He said the mirror belonged to his sister, and he's Italian. Is he Angelo? Is his sister Maria? Could this be a clue to discovering the "Poppy Flowers?"* Thoughts and questions spin through my mind. With a smile, I decide my first stop is to talk to Mr. Bell again.

2

The next morning I'm on Mr. Bell's doorstep. Nothing has changed except a small breeze blows and in the far distance I hear children playing. The sun is just as hot and the air, though it moves, smells just as stale. I lean in and knock on the door.

There's no answer so I knock again, harder. "Mr. Bell! It's Ellen Thompson! I need to speak to you!" I call loudly.

I get no answer, no response of any kind. *What to do?* I don't want to miss him and he doesn't seem to be a man who goes in public often. Is he home and just not willing to answer the door?

"Please, Mr. Bell! It's very important!" I shout.

"Damn it!" Turning from the door I place my hands on my hips. I look across and down the street, thinking. *What should my next move be?* The thought of the mirror plays in my head like a song I can't get rid of. A breeze blows debris and leaves in a swirl and a scrawny dog looks my way before he crosses the street. I shove my hair out of my face and think, *truly, it's all deserted – the street looks like a ghost town*. I wouldn't be surprised to see a tumbleweed blow past.

"What now, El?" I ask myself with a shake of my head.

I round the side of the house to the mostly nonexistent driveway. I'm not sure what I'm thinking, but I'm moving on instinct. The garage is as old and beaten up as the house and in the back the aged fence sags inward with its gate gone. I stop by the garage and, rising on my toes, peer into a small, battered window high on the overhead door. The garage is mostly empty. It has a few boxes but no car, so Mr. Bell could simply be out for a drive.

I turn to the yard. The grass has long ago given up its battle with the weeds and what trees there are appear ancient and about to fall down.

I walk into the back yard and look around. *Am I really going to do this?* I think with trepidation. *Am I really going to try and get into this house where I don't want to be on the assumption I'll get more information...*

Digging in my purse I pull out a picture of Van Gogh's "Poppy Flowers" I printed last night. It's a beautiful painting: yellow and red poppies in a vase. The painting is small, only a foot by a foot, but compelling all the same. I stare at it, nod my head and sigh, "Yeah. Yeah, I'm gonna do this."

I step around some garbage, walk up the rickety steps to the back door and reach out and try the knob.

"Well, at least it's not breaking and entering," I mutter as the knob turns and the door opens.

"Whew! Smells even worse today!" I whisper as a wave of stench causes me to catch my breath mid-inhale. I push the door open and step inside.

With a quick scan around the kitchen, I think, *Mr. Bell, you are no Martha Stewart.* The kitchen is filthy really filthy. Dirty dishes litter old counters with years of filth that'll never come off. A mixture of debris that's part old food containers, newspapers and wrappings cover the faded tiles of the floor and bugs move among the garbage. At the windows hang old drapes so tattered I can see through them. With a blink and a shake of my head, I note they are covered in faded roosters. I step over more garbage and around the kitchen table and chairs. I hear the skitter of insects and attempt to not think about the germs as I inhale keeping my breaths shallow. Approaching the hall to the rest of the house I push through the swinging door. It squeals and the smell intensifies, making me gag.

"This is so not good," I say under my breath. I screw my courage on and raise my voice to yell into the house. "Mr. Bell! It's Ellen Thompson. Can I speak to you a moment, sir?" I stop and listen intently but there's no answer; the house is eerily quiet. The only sound is the breeze that blows through the tops of the trees in the back yard like a distant freight train. With my adrenaline spiked and my breath increasing to a pant, my heart rate accelerates. In the living room the curtains are drawn. Sunlight attempts to sneak in around the edges so the room has a twilight quality. Though the house wasn't clean yesterday, it's worse today. It's torn apart, trashed! *Has it been searched?* Seat cushions are ripped open, furniture is overturned and on the floor in the corner of the room sits Mr. Bell with a hole in his forehead.

Now he's really stinky.

The next thing I realize, I'm standing bent over in the back yard gasping for breath and gagging. My eyes water and I can't catch my breath. I don't even remember leaving the house; all I see are stars.

Come on, Girl! Pull it together. This is not the place for your first faint: face down in the weeds! Placing my hands on my knees I take big gulps of air. Slowly I straighten. As I get my breath back, I stare off in the distance and try to decide what to do. Obviously, I should call the police. Mr. Bell is dead, and by the neat little hole in his forehead it's safe to say he was murdered. I hesitate, and a part of me wonders if the information I want was found by the person or persons responsible for Mr. Bell's untimely death. Maybe it's still in the house. Is there information in there which pertains to the "Poppy Flowers?" I peer over my shoulder and wonder, *would it really hurt to look before I call in* the *authorities? Did I really want to go back into the house?* I'm here, after all — I've already been in there. What could it hurt? And if I don't, if I pack it in and go home now I'll never know if the information is right there, just feet away. I'm not sure I can live with that. To be the one to find a missing masterpiece, to be there first hand and see it. It's not like I've never seen or been right up next to great works of art. I work with and around them every day. Hell the DIA is in possession of the first Van Gogh on American soil, so I'm not an ignorant groupie or something; but still — a missing Master, one that no one knows the location of, the mystery's too much for me to turn away from. In my head I can hear my father: *Ellen, your curiosity and persistence to an end will either make you a success or get you in trouble.* I run my finger over my medallion and think, *this promises to qualify for the latter, Daddy.* With a straightening of my shoulders, I pull my courage together and turn toward the house.

"Just don't look in the corner," I tell myself as I walk to the open back door, peer in, hesitating. I take a deep calming breath, walk through the kitchen, down the hall and back into the living room — mumbling, "No corner, nothing in the corner…"

Dropping my bag by the living room doorway, I take a quick scan of the room and purposefully avoid Mr. Bell. Since the mirror was in the bureau I decide to check it first. Whoever trashed the house did a fine job of taking the bureau apart. With sorrow I realize no amount of time and love can save it now. The back is broken and most of the drawers are pulled out and strewn about the room. I squat to sift through the spilled contents and pick up and read papers. I look for the names Maria and Angelo or anything that might have to do with the painting. My search includes looking under drawer areas and knocking on side panels to search for hidden compartments just like in movies, but I find nothing. I turn my attention to the rest of the living room.

As the house gets warmer, the smell becomes unbearable. With inspiration, I pull my designer scarf over my mouth and nose in an attempt to stop the urge to gag. "I bet they didn't anticipate this when marketing the scarf at Nordstrom's," I mumble to myself. I soon have sweat running down the small of my back and am increasingly uncomfortable. I find nothing of interest in the living room so I fortify myself and turn my attention to the body of Mr. Bell. *If it was important, wouldn't he keep it on himself?* I wonder. "Well, Mr. Bell?" I say out loud to his body in the corner, "what secrets might you hold?"

I move over debris and approach the body. After better securing my scarf I kneel beside him. He appears as if he's simply slid down the wall, except for a smear of blood and other matter streaking behind him that has turned a dark brown color. His body is slumped over and is held up by a table in the corner. He has on the same clothing from yesterday. Even though I don't know anything about this type of thing, if I had to guess, I would say he was hit more than once before he was killed. Due to death, his skin has a weird grayish hue but I swear there are bruises. I wonder when he was killed. Who would do this to an old crazy, seemingly harmless man? Have I just missed his assailant? I tell myself to get a move on and get out of here!

"Where to begin? Where to begin?" I mumble under my breath. I try not to look at his face — and the hole in his head — as I reach out. Surprised, I notice how much my hands shake. Turning them over and back, I peer at them like they belong to another person. I clench my fists, relaxing them again. I reach for Mr. Bell and feel the outside of his pockets. Nothing — they feel empty. Getting bolder, I place my fingers in his pants pockets and shirt pockets. I feel down his chest and legs but nothing seems out of the ordinary — other than the fact he's dead and definitely beginning to stiffen up. *Icky*, I think with a shiver. With the thought he may have a wallet in a back pocket, I stand. Taking as deep a breath as I can, I bend to grab his ankles with the plan to flip him over. The flesh gives in a disgusting way and I shiver with revulsion. I take a hold of him, lift his legs and move him. With a squeak, I drop his legs and jump back, catching my momentum so I don't fall. Mr. Bell's body moves like a piece of heavy wood. "Oh my God, oh my God! I'm gonna be sick," I mutter as I bend and try to calm down. "Keep it together, Girl! Pockets, wallet; get it done!" With determination, I squat next to his body again. I feel Mr. Bell's back pockets. Nothing! His back pockets are empty. Standing, I feel like stomping my foot. I look at his body. "Damn it! What now?"

When I step back from his body, it shifts and I notice Mr. Bell's right hand is in a tight fist. As I move closer, I touch his pale and slightly swollen skin with my fingertips. I move his hand and attempt to open his fist. He's very, very stiff and gulping, I catch a hysterical laugh in my throat as the words 'death grip' play in my mind. I stand and rub my forehead with the back of my wrist, momentarily stumped. I want to see what's in his hand. What's so important to keep a tight hold of even in death, but I don't know when he was murdered and so don't know when he'll loosen up again, and I REALLY don't want to chance breaking his fingers.

Squatting next to Mr. Bell, I take his hand in both of mine and apply increasingly strong pressure to his fingers and thumb. I hope it isn't too much pressure. *Please don't be too much*, I think, praying I don't break anything. As I continue with added pressure, there's an audible pop which surprises and revolts me and I'm able to slightly open his fist. With a small sickly grimace, I retrieve a bronze skeleton key.

Standing, I move backwards and look at the key in my hand. It's not very large, just slightly bigger than a regular key, and I have absolutely no idea what it opens.

Across the room at the doorway, I stoop and pick up my bag. I put the key in a small pocket of my billfold. What should I do now? I can't stomach the thought of staying in this house any longer. Should I call the police? Go home? I can't let Mr. Bell lie where he is. "But let's not be too stupid, El Old Girl." I feel like a criminal as I re-approach Mr. Bell's body. I grasp his ankles and heave him back to his original position.

"Sorry, Mr. Bell. I'll get someone here soon to take care of you," I assure him. Somehow, it makes me feel better to speak to him.

I step out into the back yard from the kitchen. Relieved, I move down the stairs and untied my scarf from my head. The sunshine is warm and the breeze washes over me. "Ah! Fresh-ish air." I say with a hint of sarcasm. I look down at myself and shake my head in despair. "I'm going to have to throw this entire outfit away. Dang! And I liked this shirt." With a deep breath of the hot, dry air I pull my cell phone from my purse to dial 911.

"Emergency. Please hold," says the voice on the other end of the line. With a roll of my eyes, I think, *Wow! Really?* For patience, I take a deep breath, round the house and walk toward the front yard. A moment later a woman comes on the phone.

"Detroit 911. What's your emergency?"

3

I'm sitting patiently on the front step when a blue and white police cruiser and an unmarked sedan pull up. I know I smell of Mr. Bell and the house and would really like a shower. I stand as the uniformed officers' jump out and approach me.

"Ms. Thompson?" the blond officer says as he walks to me.

"Yes," I answer, "I'm Ellen Thompson."

He stops in front of me and looking up slightly asks, "You called about a DB?"

With a confused look and a shake of my head, I ask, "DB?"

"Oh, sorry Ma'am. A dead body."

"Oh, yes, yes." I have to wrinkle my nose at the term. "Mr. Bell is inside. It looks like his home has been robbed and he's been shot. The back door is unlocked."

"Ok, Ma'am. Please wait here, we'll check it out." The officer gestures to his partner and they head around the side of the house. I'm drained and it's difficult to breathe. All I can think about is a bubble bath and a glass — no make that a bottle — of wine.

"Ms. Thompson?" says a deep voice behind me.

Startled and with a little jump, I turn and look up. My mind goes blank except for one big thought: *WOW! PRETTY!*

The detective is dressed in a gray suit, he's middle-aged and probably 6'2" with short salt and pepper hair and intense eyes.

"Ms. Thompson?" he repeats and looks down at me.

"Um? Yes, oh yes. Um, I'm Ellen Thompson." I stammer like an imbecile and mentally shake myself.

"I'm Detective Russell." He gestures to the other man, "This is my partner Detective Boyd. We'd like to ask you some questions. Would it be possible for you to come down to the station?"

With another mental shake, I say "Yes, of course." I pull my gaze from Detective Russell and look at the other man. Detective Boyd is older, maybe in his 50s, shorter and a bit squat. He gives me a small smile and a nod. As I glance between the men I nod my head and say, "Yes, of course. That would be fine."

"We'll secure the location and be right behind you. Just tell the sergeant on duty you're meeting with us and he'll let you know where to wait."

I nod my understanding.

*****

The police station appears busy and quite imposing with cop cars parked out front and uniformed officers coming and going. I've never had reason to be in the station before and feel a little intimidated. With my bag firmly on my shoulder, I head up the stairs. I pull open the glass door and I'm hit by a wall of noise. The inside of the police station is a mass of hustling people who all talk at once and the volume is deafening. It's an older brick building that does a poor job of funneling the human traffic. People shuffle around each other, bumping and jostling back and forth. After I approach him and explain my situation, the Sergeant tells me to have a seat and wait. I sigh and wish I'd just walked away when I had the chance. I make my way through the crowd and find a seat against one wall. The chair is hard and plastic and I shift repeatedly in an attempt to get comfortable. *Apparently, they don't want people to want to stay*, I think with a grimace. As my stomach growls, I make a face. *Really? After today? I think I may never eat again.*

The flow of noise and energy subtly shifts and Detective Russell heads toward me through the sea of people. He's pretty easy to notice since he's the tallest person in the room. I watch him move through the crowd, and they move out of his way without any guidance from him. It makes me wonder if it's his size or the authority he projects.

JAMES

Detective Russell heads to the sergeant to see where he put Ellen Thompson when she arrived, but then spots her across the room where she avidly observes people. He doesn't understand what it is about her that makes him react so strongly. She's beautiful, but he knows many beautiful women. All he knows is he will need to control it — at least until she's cleared of murder.

ELLEN

As he nears, I get to my feet and wait for him. I enjoy the rush of attraction and anticipation I feel, it's a heady combination. My skin flushes and my breath quickens. As he approaches, Detective Russell's facial features become sterner and sterner. He stops and looks down. With my height, it's not often that anyone looks down at me and I like the false feeling of frailty.

"Ms. Thompson, please follow me."

Turning with him, I think, *Anywhere*. A small smile curves my lips and I mutter to myself. "Getting rummy, El!"

Detective Russell leads me to a small interrogation room. I figure Detective Boyd is watching this interview behind the mirror or on a screen somewhere.

The room's an institutional shade of mustard yellow. The paint is chipped on the back concrete wall next to the mirror. In the center of the room is a metal table with two chairs on either side. The table has a large U shaped bar bolted to it. Somehow, the table makes me nervous and a little guilty; why can I imagine myself handcuffed to it? Even though a small breath of air conditioning spits out a vent, the room is warm and I'm conscience of my own mix of odors and hope Detective Russell isn't aware. I stare at the table as he says, "Please have a seat." He walks past me and pulls out the chair closest to me then moves around the table to sit in one of the chairs on the opposite side

Keep on your toes, Girl! I think as I sit. This chair is as hard and uncomfortable as the one in the reception area. It seems everything in the station is hard.

"Would you like some water or coffee, Ms. Thompson?" Detective Russell asks me.

"No thank you."'

I try to relax. Although I haven't done anything wrong, I still didn't call emergency right away, I moved the body and searched the room. Not entirely innocent. I'm guilty and jumpy but attempt to project a calm face. I sit quietly, look at Detective Russell and wait.

"Ms. Thompson, did you know the deceased well?"

As he looks at me I catch Detective Russell's eyes and realize they're a deep clear blue. Beautiful.

"Ms. Thompson," he repeats.

"Oh — um? I'm sorry," I blink rapidly, "No, not really. I met Mr. Bell yesterday. I purchased a reproduction 1920s hand mirror from him."

"A mirror?" He looks at me with doubt.

"Yes, I found him on Craigslist. I originally thought the mirror was vintage, but when I got there I realized it wasn't. We were able to come to an agreement about the price. I met him at his home yesterday and purchased it."

"You bought the hand mirror?"

I nod my head, "Yes, for $50. It's quite lovely."

"This was yesterday."

"Yes, yesterday afternoon, about 2:00." Detective Russell makes notations on a pad in front of him. Curious what he wrote, I sit up straight and lean forward, attempting to read his chicken scratch upside down. As he looks up, Detective Russell catches my eye and I smile a little sheepishly at him, but when he doesn't return my smile, mine slowly melts from my face. *Why won't he warm up?*

The detective blinks, looks back at his pad of paper and asks me, "Why were you at Mr. Bell's house today?"

I hesitate. I don't want to mention the note in the mirror or the key I'd found.

With a quick thought, I say, "Um…Mr. Bell told me he had the matching hair brush to sell, but that I'd need to come back today."

Detective Russell narrows his eyes and gives me a doubtful look. "Uh huh. You must have wanted it pretty bad. Neighbors reported you banged on his front door and were yelling."

"Well, I wouldn't say that," I reply self-consciously. "He assured me the brush was beautiful and I guess I really wanted it."

"So when no one answered the front door you thought you'd try the back?"

I nod my head in agreement. "He did say he'd be home and so I went around to the back. The door was unlocked."

Detective Russell looks at me like he's studying me.

"Did you ever wonder why a man like Mr. Bell would have a vintage brush and mirror set?"

"He said it belonged to his sister," I say with a shrug.

Detective Russell glances at his notes then looks up and leans forward. "Ms. Thompson, do you own a gun?"

"Wwhaat?" I stutter with amazement. "A gun? No, No. I've never even held a gun." My whole body breaks out in a sweat. I lean back from the table and with a dizzy feeling remind myself to breathe; just breathe. I blink rapidly at him and ask, "Am I a suspect?"

Detective Russell continues to study me. "At this time, Ma'am we're exploring all possibilities." His face is blank and his voice is very professional. "Ms. Thompson, we would like to get a DNA sample from you and check your hands and clothes for gunshot residue. It's really a formality. A process of elimination, if you will. Would you willingly comply with this request?"

I know I've done nothing wrong. I haven't shot Mr. Bell so I have no problem being accommodating with the police and want to make their jobs easier, but first I ask quietly "Do I need a lawyer?" I find myself wishing more and more that I hadn't called the police.

"That, of course, is your right, but you aren't under arrest."

I know my father would be ashamed of me if I denied the police my help. I reach to touch my medallion and nod my head, "Of course, of course. Take what you need."

Detective Russell's eyebrows shoot up at my easy acquiescence and he stares at me for a moment. He nods at the mirror then turns back to me. "A tech will be right in." I glance at the mirror and realize I was right — Detective Boyd is observing the interview.

JAMES

As he watches Ellen Thompson, Detective Russell thinks maybe he should have let Boyd do this interview. It's obvious to him that his attraction has colored his responses. In an attempt to not show her favoritism, he's concerned he might be acting too harsh, too stoic.

There's a soft knock on the door and it opens to admit a short, older woman. She sets a brown leather case on the table. All business, she opens the case and withdraws a swab. She asks Ellen to wipe it on the inside of her cheek. After she's done so, Ellen hands it back to her where she places it in a sealed tube in her case. The technician moistens another cloth and wipes it over Ellen's hands. She places a few drops of a different liquid on it and puts it in a container.

Ellen complies with the technician but continues to watch Detective Russell as the process takes place. He watches her as she watches him and begins to feel like he's being judged.

ELLEN

Through the process with the lab technician, I scrutinize Detective Russell and feel more and more as if he has let me down. I don't understand my feelings, I barely know him, but the feelings are there all the same. When the tech is done, she closes her case, nods at Detective Russell and walks out, quietly closing the door. The entire process had a surreal quality I can't shake.

I steel myself and look him directly in the face. "Detective Russell, do you have any other questions for me? I'd like to go home."

"Not right now, Ms. Thompson. Please stay available and don't leave town."

As he stands, I take the hint. I jump up and push my chair back to head for the door. Detective Russell reaches around me and pulls the door open. As I slide past him he hands me his card. I glance at the card and put it in my purse. I wait to see if he has anything else to say.

"Please call me if you remember anything. Thank you for your cooperation."

I leave the room and walking toward the elevator, I see Detective Boyd approach. I stop out of their view and put my back to the wall. I'm eavesdropping but instead of shame it fills me with a level of power that has been taken from me.

"What do you think?" Detective Boyd asks.

"I think she's hiding something."

"Too bad. Pretty gal. Hope she's not caught up in something she can't handle."

I hear Detective Russell give a small sigh. "We'll see."

They walk away and soon I'm down the elevator and at my car. I need my home. I need to feel safe again.

JAMES

Detectives Russell and Boyd walk into the bullpen and approach their desks. The room is noisy with the sound of phones ringing and people talking. It's crowded with cops and suspects. Everyone is busy and shifts of police are coming or going. The detectives slip past desks and people as they move through the room to their area. They sit at their desks, each face the other and discuss what's next. They're a good team and work well with and respect each other. They decide they'll run Joe Bell in the system and see what pops. Detective Russell knows something is off. Ellen Thompson is withholding information, but he can't put his finger on what it might be. He knows one thing for certain; she didn't murder Joe Bell.

ELLEN

I can't get home fast enough. I'm tired and stinky and becoming short-tempered. I even flipped off a man driving too fast and recklessly. At my apartment complex I walk through the front door, look at the stairs which I always take, and turn toward the elevator.

"Not tonight, baby," I sigh. "Mama's at the end of her rope. Cabernet take me away!"

When the fourth floor pings and the elevator opens, I step out and head down the hall. I live in a nice one bedroom apartment. I have nice neighbors who, for the most part, keep to themselves. Tonight I wish they hadn't.

At my door I dig through my purse for my keys. As I put the key in the hole and turn the handle, the door opens on its own. Standing for a moment, I stare at the door that's slightly ajar before my brain wakes up. With a push on the door I crane my neck to peer inside. I see my apartment and think, *Well, SHIT. This day ain't over yet.* As I back out my door and head for the elevator, I dig for my phone and the card Detective Russell gave me.

The call is answered by a decidedly grumpy voice. "Detective Russell," he says. In the background I hear people talking and phones ringing.

I assume he's still at the station and say, "Hello, Detective Russell, this is Ellen Thompson. I hope you don't mind I called you. I have a problem."

4

When Detectives Russell and Boyd arrive at the apartment building I'm waiting for them in the reception area on the main floor. I stand as they enter the building. I'm totally beat and certain I look it. Detective Russell looks at me and there's a softening of his features. I feel myself respond to him all over again.

"Ms. Thompson," he says quietly.

"Detective Russell, Detective Boyd," I look at them both with gratitude. "Thank you for coming so quickly. I stayed out of my apartment like you said."

"Good. Let's have a look."

I'm torn between the wish that this day would end and that it never would — with the grumpy Detective Russell here I'm feeling safer, calmer. I shake my head in confusion and mutter to myself, "Ah, El. How sick are you. Girlfriend, you need some sleep."

We reach my apartment and Detective Boyd asks me to stay in the hallway. As he and Detective Russell pull their weapons, I step backward, my eyes wide. They push open the door and enter the premises.

"Detroit Police! Come out with your hands up!"

There's no answer of bullets or voices and I hear them move around. The apartment seems to be empty. When I peek in the door, I see what made me back out an hour ago. My living room is ripped apart.

"Damn," I sigh. This is definitely a low point in my life. *Even worse than when Tommy Wilson dumped me in seventh grade*, I think in an attempt to cheer up. I hear the detectives in the far reaches of my apartment as they check for intruders, so I walk into what used to be my home.

"Damn." Everything is torn up. My books are strewn about. Furniture is ripped up. Even food is thrown all over. Really? Food? What bastard has to fling last night's General Tso's Chicken around? What did my dinner ever do to him? Now my apartment has an overwhelming scent of soy. I pick up the remnants of a porcelain figurine I got in France a few years ago. It used to be a Kings Cake Figurine of a little shepherd boy, but now it's simply garbage. My heart turns over with the loss of just this one keepsake and I'm afraid to take a good look around at my belongings. Detectives Russell and Boyd come out of the bedroom. Detective Boyd pulls out his phone and calls in the break-in.

"Well, it looks like whoever did this is long gone." With a searching look Detective Russell adds, "Maybe you want to tell us what this is all about?"

What do I want to tell him? I wish I could have some down time and get some sleep to get my wits about me again. I'm suspicious of my need to trust him so quickly. I want to know where it comes from, to understand it before I act on it — if I do.

With a decision made, I say, "I have no idea what you are talking about." I'm proud of myself as I stay straight-faced and innocent looking.

"Uh huh. I'm supposed to believe this has nothing to do with Mr. Bell's death today?" He looks as if he'd like to shake me. Even frustration looks good on him.

With an angelic, wide-eyed stare I say, "I don't see how it can. I barely knew him." I shake my head. "This must be some random coincidence." Detective Russell stares at me. He doesn't say anything but skepticism is plain on his face.

"I've got a unit heading down to secure the apartment and get any information from the scene," Detective Boyd says as he comes back into the room. "Do you have anywhere else you can stay tonight?"

I look at Detective Boyd and then stare at Detective Russell. As I turn away, I say, "Let me grab a few items, please. I'll stay at a hotel."

As he walks away Detective Russell mutters, "Damn women."

*****

Sitting on the bed in my hotel room in a white terrycloth robe and freshly washed hair I sip red wine from a hotel glass. I'm drained. I don't know what to do. Should I tell Detective Russell the truth? — At least the truth as I know it? In my hand are the note and the key and I'm trying to decide where to go from here. Tomorrow I'm definitely going to have to deal with my apartment but tonight I'll finish my business with the mirror. I log onto my email and wait for it to update. Right away, amongst the garbage of ads and other internet flotsam, I notice an email from the account on Craigslist I used for correspondence with Mr. Bell. I sit and stare at it, waiting for it to jump out and bite me and for a moment I can't bring myself to click on it — this man is dead. The email was delivered yesterday, about midafternoon. It was after I'd purchased the mirror. Why did he email me? I pace around the hotel room, agitated, sipping wine.

"Ok, El. Guess there's only one way to know what this is about." I set my wine down on the bedside table and crawl onto the bed. Pulling my laptop closer, I click on the email from Mr. Bell and watch as it expands on the screen.

"**Ms. Thompson**," it begins and I can almost hear his wispy, scratchy voice.

"Thank you for your purchase of my sister's mirror today. It was a pleasure to meet with you."

I reread this portion twice since it seems so sane and businesslike. Not at all like the Mr. Bell I met. Perhaps he had periods of sanity and after I left he emailed me during one of these times.

"As I stated, the mirror was my sister's and as was usual, her possessions held many secrets. After you left I realized I have other items you might be interested in, items of the same caliber and subject matter – if you have inspected the mirror you know what I speak of. These items and what they represent are no longer of any interest to me and I wish to discard them. You might be better equipped to find interest and truth in all her possessions and where they may lead you. I can no longer stand to look at them and have moved her box into my garage for the time being. Please let me know if you are interested as I will throw the cursed things out in the trash as soon as possible. I would warn you, the items carry a darkness that emanates from my sister and has settled in her belongings. If I were you, I would stay as far away from them as possible but I understand the call of a mystery. They are yours if you want them."

I read the email for the third time and think maybe he doesn't sound as sane as I thought. There's definitely weirdness to his words and confusion to reality. Where did the key come in, or did it? Did it mean anything? I'm not so tired after all. I throw on a pair of black jeans, a navy shirt and comfortable boots. I grab my bag to hurry downstairs. As I get to my car, I consider the layout of the Bell property. I've looked into the garage, looked for a car, and seen a few stacks of items. I hope there won't be a reason for a police presence around the house, but just the same, I'll show caution.

After climbing into my car, I drive to the general location of Mr. Bell's house. I decide to park a couple blocks away. In silence, I spend the time rehashing all the information I have. What other items might I find in the garage? Do Mr. Bell's cryptic comments about the subject matter of the items and secrets have to do with the note I found in the mirror? What's this all about? Why does he have his sister's belongings?

When I arrive downtown, I park on the street and get out. I lock my car with a fleeting thought that perhaps this side of town, this time of night isn't the best choice but running full tilt into situations is something I do quite well. Ignoring my disquiet, I head toward Mr. Bell's house. The neighborhood is almost silent, even now it feels deserted. Funny, because I know it isn't. Not only did Mr. Bell live here, but Detective Russell said neighbors heard me at his door. There's a minimal amount of illumination from old street lamps that still function, kind of. They aren't very bright, just bright enough to have moths fluttering around. I feel nervous but also keyed up and adventurous. The nights always make me feel this way. I walk by his house and monitor it from the corner of my eye, but keep going. I round the corner and go down the alley and approach from the back of the property. The fence is no obstacle since it's practically nonexistent and I easily push through an open area. Once inside the fence, I stop and listen. I hear dogs in the distance and the hum of the highway. A breeze blows and it feels good against my hot skin. I tip my face into it, and allow a moment for the sweat to dry and calm to settle. As I approach the garage, I stop, listening. Nothing. No one. The house, garage and yard are dark and quiet. All I hear is the sound of a lone cricket as it calls to a mate. I try the door and am surprised when the knob turns and the door opens. I shut the door behind me. The interior is dark and musky with stale air. There are shapes along the walls and a smell of old motor oil and dust. I wait a moment to be certain nothing will happen and then reach into my bag and find the small flashlight I keep for emergencies. I shield the illumination with my hand and body. The garage is lit with the partial, distilled light. There's a small cardboard box against the back wall. It appears to have been moved recently to this area since there isn't any dust on it.

It's unsealed, so I squat down and open it. It contains a few postcards and a pretty little box that proves to be a music box. The top, which has a four heart design, opens and has compartments inside. When I wind the key on the bottom, it plays a pretty melody. It seems familiar, seems to tug a cord in my memory. Deciding to take the entire cardboard box with me, I turn the switch to stop the music box from playing and place it back in the box. I fold the top into itself, pick it up and set it by the door. There doesn't seem to be anything else of interest or even out of the ordinary. I look over the array of tools, old cans of paint and weed killer — the latter two obviously haven't been used in quite a while. There's nothing else here so I retrieve the key that was in Mr. Bell's hand from my front pocket. As I near the garage door, I turn off the flashlight and put it back in my bag. With the door open I try the key in it. Nope, it won't fit. I put the key back into my pocket, pick up my bag and the box. I open the door wider and stop, listening to the night. Distant dogs, crickets and the cool smell of darkness. As I step across the threshold, I quietly pull the door closed and traverse back the way I came, across the back yard, out the fence and down the alley. Two blocks down, I approach my car. Once I unlock it, I place the box in the backseat and drive away.

Back at the hotel, with the box and standing next to my car, I look around the parking lot. I'm not sure what I'm expecting, but I'm like a criminal on a covert mission. A mission that so far, has been a success.

Heading into the hotel I feel as if the eyes of the world are on me. In the elevator I take a deep breath of relief. I hold tight to the box, feeling like someone is going to take it from me before I can investigate it. I can hardly wait to get back to my room and look at the contents. What item could Mr. Bell have meant for me to look at? What did he think I might be interested in and how did it pertain to the note? He talked of secrets and darkness. He was right, a mystery is hard to refuse and I'm anxious to see what I can find.

As I enter my hotel room the door swings shut and locks behind me. The room is quiet. I should have left the T.V. on when I went out. I place the box on the bed and stand back to look at it. Nervous now about what I might not find, I grab my phone and take the time to run a quick scan through my emails to make sure there's nothing of interest — no late arriving communication from the dead Mr. Bell. I click the T.V. on for some noise and sit to remove my boots. With my elbows on my knees, I look across the room at the box. What if it doesn't have anything of interest in it? What if I went to Mr. Bell's house for no reason? What if he was just a crazy man and my mystery ends here?

"Might as well dive in and see what's there."

I open the box and pull the few items out. There are postcards and the music box. It isn't very big, 5" x 6" maybe and the lid is attractive with the etchings of four hearts. On the bottom is the key to wind it and it says 'Made in Italy'.

"Italy again," I comment. I open it, verify it's empty and turn the key on the bottom to listen to the tune. It's a nice melody, tinny yet relaxing in the way of music boxes.

"What is that song?" I question aloud. "I'm sure I know that song." I hum a little to try and refresh my memory but it alludes me, so I set the music box on the bedside table. I continue to listen as I look at the cards. They're from different spots on the globe and don't seem to have any relationship to each other. I'm not sure what I'm supposed to see but I do know I'm missing it. I feel the fog of exhaustion come over me and I'm concerned I'll miss something if I continue tonight, so I place everything in the box and put it on the floor.

I strip to my underwear, wash my face, brush and floss my teeth, rewind the music box and climb into bed. I lay looking at the box for a moment and then, yawning, reach across it to turn off the bedside lamp. In the darkness I lay and listen to the music play as I drift to sleep.

5

I jerk at a loud boom but don't know where I am! Frantically, I look left and right, searching for something, anything I recognize but only see smoke and ash. I feel ephemeral, weightless and realize not only can I not see through the haze, but I can't smell anything. A tune plays gently in the distance.

Suddenly, there's another large boom and the earth shakes. Thrusting out my hands, I bend at the waist to catch my balance as the earth shifts. Figures, half seen in the smoke, run past me but make no sound. Where am I? What's happening? I squat to the road I'm on. Reaching out, I touch the paving stones. They feel real enough. They're hard, rough and warm. As I stand and move forward blindly, I glimpse a wall of a building coming into view. I lay my hand upon a wall of red stucco and marble and note the beauty and vibrancy of color. In the smoke and haze it's the only color I can detect. The explosions continue to sound and I see a huge plume of smoke, debris and ash and an intense wave of heat heads toward me. With the wall of heat comes clarity as the smoke is driven aside and I'm able to see the immense volcano erupt a few miles away. I look into hell on earth and flatten myself against the trembling wall as the furnace of heat washes over me.

I awake with a start and sit straight up in bed. I know the song.

I went up this evening, Nanetta
Do you know where? Do you know where?
Where your hard heart can't reach
With scornful wiles! With scornful wiles!
Where the fire burns, but if you run
You can escape it! You can escape it!
It doesn't chase you nor destroy you
Just by a look. Just by a look.

I look at the postcard in my hand. I'm stunned. I read the lyrics again and continue to the body of the card as I pace around the room.

Maria

I came to this place thinking it might help me burn the memory of you from my mind but still you are everywhere I look. I feel our passion in the heat, your whisper of 'I love you' in the wind. Why won't you give me some peace? How far will I need to travel? I tried to not contact you, but your face is the only real thing I have – but always there is the 'Poppies'; calling to me...

I send this card with a package — a present to you.

Remember me, my love.

    Angelo

When I finish reading the postcard I regard the music box that's again playing its tune. When I woke, I'd jumped up and rummaged through the cardboard box. I looked for a card I'd seen. Finding it, I studied the photo on the front: Mount Vesuvius in Italy. That's why the tune is so familiar.

A few months ago while surfing through the channels on my TV, feeling bored and a bit out of sorts, I'd come across a special on Mount Vesuvius and the city of Pompeii. I've always thought the story of Pompeii compelling, so when it caught my attention I let it run while I finished cleaning. Before I knew it, I'd sat in front of the TV and raptly watched the show. There was a small part, just a sidebar really, on a rail car built to the top of Mount Vesuvius. When the rail car, or funicular I remember they called it, opened for business people across Italy were so excited a man wrote a song. The tune played in the background and is the tune that plays right now.

Wide awake, I return to the box. I search for another mention of Pompeii, Mount Vesuvius or Naples. Angelo must have travelled to Naples or Mount Vesuvius after he left Maria. What crazy need drove him there? It seems the package he sent must have been the music box. That was an assumption, but one I am willing to make based on the song from the music box and his post card. His writing confirms his possession of the 'Poppies' at that location.

I set the card on the bedside table and pick up the music box. The Buzz hits like a lightning bolt. I looked it over last night but hadn't found anything of interest. There hadn't been any feelings to indicate it was special. I open the lid, close the lid, turn it over, wind the key, and shake it. Nothing. It's just a simple wooden music box. I pace the floor and give the box a good shake. Suddenly I stop and shake the music box again, really hard and move it closer to my ear.

I catch my breath... There it is! Something is loose in the box. It moves around when I shake it. I spin around excitedly to face the room, in a dilemma. I open the lid and pull at the insides. I twist and turn them in an attempt to open it. Nothing budges.

"Dang it!" I breathe, frustrated.

Without forethought, I lift the music box above my head and smash it to the ground where it shatters into shards. The music assembly skitters across the room and I hear a small *tinkle* as a piece ricochets across the floor and under a bedside table. Dropping to my hands and knees, I crawl forward and lay my cheek on the floor to peer under the table. In the light of the room, a small glint reflects off a golden key. I reach under the table, leery, almost as if it might disappear. I grasp the key and pull my hand back. With my prize retrieved, I sit on my haunches and open my hand.

The key is small. There's a set of numbers on one side and a symbol on the other. It looks like a mermaid with something written above it. I need my magnifying lens, and my lens is in my apartment. "Looks like it's time to head home and face cleaning that mess."

With the shards of the music box placed in the cardboard box, I pull my belongings together. It's early, but there's no reason to delay getting home and cleaning things up and while there, I can further investigate the key.

6

JAMES

That morning, Detectives Russell and Boyd look at each other over the dead body of Joe Bell. As of yet, they've found no evidence he existed prior to about four years ago. No history of any kind: priors, voting records, family history or anything before he showed up in America on a flight from Italy.

"So it appears he was beaten prior to being shot?" Detective Boyd asks the Medical Examiner.

"Yes, he has severe contusions about his head and upper body consistent with prolonged physical abuse. I also located two fingers that were broken; possibly post mortem," the ME answers. "The COD is a gunshot to the head, which is obvious. It's a small caliber — .22, but fired point blank. He has GSR on the skin and bruising around the wound."

"I wonder if whoever did this got what they were after. We haven't found anything out of the ordinary in his home — the techs are still sifting through his belongings," Detective Boyd comments.

Detective Russell can't get the thought of Ellen Thompson out of his head. What was she doing at Joe Bell's? What did she know? What kind of trouble has she gotten herself into? He knows she's in danger but isn't sure she will welcome his help. "Thank you, Doctor. Please keep us informed if you come up with anything else."

ELLEN

I'm not sure what I'll find when I get back to my apartment.

Wow, What a mess! I walk further into the room and as I step over a mixture of some of my broken treasures and pieces of destroyed furniture, everything crunches underfoot. A cloud of self-pity closes in and I try to shake it off.

I move to the kitchen, open a drawer and pull out my magnifying glass. I take the key from my pocket and peer at it through the glass. I'm right, the image is a mermaid. She appears to be sitting on rocks with water in front of her, maybe brushing her hair? Above the image, very faintly etched is the word PARTHENOPE.

"Parthenope?" I say with a scowl, "Never heard of it..."

I avoid the debris strewn about and retrieve my laptop, which I'd set down upon entering the apartment. Pushing items aside, I sit on the couch and fire up my computer. When Bing comes on-line I enter 'Parthenope'. It only takes a moment for multiple items to pop. There was a Greek siren, a university, a crab...I keep looking and BAM! There it is. Parthenope is the patron of Naples, Italy. I read about the woman whose very name means Love and am flabbergasted! This has to be what the image on the key is about — I don't know what or why or what it means but considering the key was in a music box playing a tune about Mount Vesuvius and has an image and name of the patron of Naples, it has to go together.

My mind is spinning. What next? What does the key go to? What will I find? Where should I go and what should I do? Should I go or do anything? Was I being impetuous and stupid? Was I putting myself in danger?

I decide to clean my apartment while I mull over these questions. I put my chin up and tell myself, "I'd better jump in and see what can get accomplished, huh?"

✶✶✶✶✶

I've cleaned for hours and made good progress. Most of the broken items are thrown away and I've found a few treasures that survived the break-in. They're sitting in a place of honor on a shelf and I glance at them periodically to bolster my spirit. Partway through the day I stop and call in an order to Mai's Chinese Cuisine down the street and have it delivered. I thought a little homage to my General Tao's Chicken's was in order. I eat my lunch and think, *one good thing is I'm finally going to have a reason for replacing my couch*!

"See," I say out loud, "I can be optimistic."

After I eat, I jump back in and really make headway. I've just come back to my apartment from the trash and turn in a circle to figure out what to do next when there's a knock at the door. I peek through the peep hole and see Detective Russell. With a secret smile I wonder what's up with him. Why might he stop by? Maybe he knows something about Joe Bell's murder. I open the door, but stand in the doorway and gaze up at him. "Detective Russell, to what do I owe this pleasure?" And it is a pleasure. If possible, he's even better looking today. He wears a black suit and the dark color really suits him. It sets off the pepper part of his salt and pepper hair and makes the blue in his eyes stand out.

"Ms. Thompson," he says with a small nod. "How are you doing today?"

"I'm well, thank you. What can I do for you? Do you have any information about Mr. Bell?"

"No, Ma'am," he answers. "In fact, he's a bit of a mystery. May I come in?"

I open the door wide and step out of the way to let him enter the apartment. With an athletic stride he walks to the middle of the room, circles, pushes back the front of his jacket and places his hands on his hips. He nods with appreciation at what I've accomplished. I smile at him since his actions mirror mine from just moments ago. "It's looking better," he states, and smiles.

"Yes, but I don't think I'll stay here for another night. Truthfully, I'm a bit freaked out about having been broken into like this." I glance around my apartment and shiver. I wonder if I'll ever feel truly at home here again.

"Ms. Thompson," he begins. "I came by on official business. I'm happy to tell you you've been cleared as a suspect in the Bell Murder. Your story checks out and with no GSR or DNA evidence you're free to resume your normal activities." I raise my eyebrows. "You never were a serious suspect, Ms. Thompson but we needed to cross all the T's and dot all the I's. I hope you understand."

"Yes, Detective Russell, I completely understand." I'm relieved to hear this news for obvious reasons but think, *Thank God,* because while I cleaned I decided what I'm going to do about the mystery of the painting and the new question of the key and Naples.

I'm going to do it! I'm going to follow Angelo's trail. I'll jump in with both feet and let my brain and instincts guide me and if it ends up being nothing more than an adventure, then I'll have the memories to look back on and smile. I take another quick scan of the room and Detective Russell standing in it and say, "Well? I think I'm done for the day." I start for the door, grab my bag and laptop and look over my shoulder at him, "You coming?"

JAMES

As Detective Russell watches Ellen head to the hotel he stops himself from following her and forcing her to talk to him. He knows whoever else is involved in this will go to extreme measures to get what they want. Why has it become so important so quickly that he find out everything she knows, that he make certain she's okay?

He sits in his police-issue sedan as she pulls out of the parking lot, his fingers tapping on the steering wheel as his head fills with thoughts of her. He knows almost nothing about her except what he's learned from the investigation and his first-hand conversations with her. It's possible she's innocent of anything other than the purchase of a hand mirror. But if that's the truth, why did her apartment get tossed? What were they looking for? Who were they? He needs to get some information out of her. He puts his car in gear and heads to the hotel.

ELLEN

I spin around as a knock sounds on my hotel door. I've accessed the DIA's webpage and put in for some time off. I'm one of those people who continue to accumulate vacation days and hardly ever use them. What can I say? My work is my life. As soon as I hear back from my supervisor I'll book the flight to Naples. If all goes as planned, I'll leave late the next day and fly with a layover in Venice. Once there, I'll decide whether the trail ends or if I'll be going forward.

I approach the door and peek through the peephole. Detective Russell stands outside my room. "Curiouser and curiouser," I mutter as I crack the door. "Yes? Detective Russell, how can I help you?"

"Can I come in, Ms. Thompson? We need to talk."

"Just give me a moment, please." I shut the door and scan the room a bit frantically and wonder what's going on. Why is he here? I deem the room fit for the police and smile at myself, thinking, *well, only one way to find out*. I catch the reflection of myself in the bathroom mirror and quickly fluff my hair, smiling a big smile. *No matter what, the night has improved with the presence of Detective Russell!*

"What can I help you with, Detective?"

"Ms. Thompson. Although the Detroit Police Department doesn't at this time, and really never did, consider you a suspect in the Joe Bell murder, we do feel you have information you aren't being forthcoming about."

I look at him skeptically and say, "The whole Detroit Police Department thinks this? Or is it just something you're fixated on, detective?"

"Look, Ellen, can I call you Ellen?" he says with a raised eyebrow. At my nod, he continues, "Ellen, I'm concerned you aren't taking your safety seriously…"

I interrupt him and walk forward. "Detective. I happen to take my safety very seriously, but what you forget is I don't know anything." My temper begins to rise and sweat breaks out across my forehead. "I just happened to meet Mr. Bell on his worst day, that's all. I hope you understand that."

When he just stares at me, I add, "And I'm real tired from the last few days. If you'll excuse me now, I'm going to order some food and call it a night."

He seems to want to say something else, but just stands in the middle of my hotel room. I walk by him, stop at my door and pull it open to wait for him to leave. I'm serious and not going to tell him anything else. He walks out the door and turns in the hall to look at me. "Good night, detective" I say and shut the door.

As I close the door in his face, I hear my computer ping with an incoming communication.

If I hadn't been so tired and drug out, I would have taken the time to consider the detective's concerns were valid. A man was dead and my apartment had been broken into. I may be in a situation that's putting me in danger…

7

ELLEN

When I wake the next morning I feel raring to go. I got the vacation time approved. In fact, they were excited I'm going to travel for personal reasons. After I finished with the work formalities, I got back online and booked a one way ticket for Naples, Italy via Venice.

With a smile, I acknowledge both my nerves and excitement. *What an adventure this is going to be!* First, home to pack some items and speak to my super. It'll be good he knows I'll be gone — especially after the break-in.

JAMES

Detective James Russell had a long frustrating day. Now at Ellen's apartment he plans on getting information out of her. He's done pussyfooting around the issues. He knows she knows something and he isn't going to leave without knowing it, too. He knocks on Ellen's door. After he waits for a few moments, he knocks again. *What the hell?* he thinks. *Maybe she went into work or ran to the store.* He knocks again, a little louder, and waits. Just then the door at the end of the hallway opens and a small nerdy young man peeks out. He wears a striped shirt and reminds the detective of the 'Where's Waldo' character.

"Are you looking for Ellen?" he asks.

"Yes," answers Detective Russell. "I'm a police officer and I have information about her break-in from the other night." As he speaks, Detective Russell moves toward the neighbor and shows his badge.

The man nods. "She just caught a plane."

"WHAT? Are you sure?"

"Yes, she told me as she was leaving. She asked me to keep an eye on her place."

"Did she tell you where she was going?" *What the hell is going on?* he thinks.

"Um? Somewhere in Italy, I think."

"Italy?"

"Yah. Italy, I'm pretty sure."

James puts in a call to the police station. He asks one of the computer techs to run a search on recent credit card activity in the name of Ellen Marie Thompson and gives her address. In a moment, the tech confirms the purchase of a one-way ticket to Naples, Italy.

"Damn It," he says. "She's flown the coop!"

ELLEN

I'm finally on the plane to Naples. I'm tired but also so excited. The flight from Detroit to Venice was uneventful, which was good. I sat next to a nice older lady whose husband was seated further back in the plane. They were on a vacation to Italy and she talked my ear off. But it was alright, I had to smile about it. Mrs. Costello's husband's family was originally from Italy and he was anxious to share that history with her — even though they'd been married for years, this was a new adventure for them. If I'm being truthful, I admit I'm a bit envious. I could see how much Mrs. Costello loves her husband and how excited she is for them to make this trip together.

This shorter flight proves to be as full as the overseas one and I hope the person seated next to me isn't in a talkative mood. In an attempt to ensure this, I have my magazine out on my lap and my iPod in my hand with my headphones in my ears. I don't want to be rude, but a little silence is in order. I need to figure out my next move. I've been impetuous and jumped on the plane without much thought, so now I have to figure out what to do. This flight is only a little over an hour and then I'll be faced with decisions.

With a large yawn I decide a hotel is going to be the first thing. Food, shower and sleep, then I'll see if I can locate what the key opens. I wonder what Detective Russell thought when he found out I left. With a small satisfied smile curling my lips, I imagine him seething. *Bet I've got your attention now...*

JAMES

James is still fuming that "Ms. Ellen Marie Thompson" left town, and left without telling him. Last night she was all 'I need sleep' but not even one indication she was leaving the next day. He takes a deep breath and tells himself to relax. He'll take it up with her when he sees her — and he will see her. He looks out the window of the airplane, anxious for it to get into the air. He's on a direct flight from Detroit Metropolitan Wayne County Airport to Naples, Italy. With any luck, he'll beat her to Naples.

ELLEN

Ah! This flight has been calm and quiet; just what I needed. With a small smile on my face I stand in the aisle of the airplane and grab my laptop from the overhead compartment. Stooping a little I glance out the window and am pleased to see the day appears to be nice and sunny. Barring anything else, it'll be wonderful to see Italy.

The passengers finally begin to move and I shift with them toward the front of the plane. I can tell I'm not the only one excited as people talk loudly all around me. I catch a few of their eyes and some of the conversations and smile at them. As I walk toward the baggage area, I sling my laptop bag crosswise over my body and pull my purse up on my shoulder. It's a bit of a hike to the baggage claim since Naples International is a large airport.

With a jerk, I stop at an intersection of foot traffic, spin in a circle and look around. I feel as if I'm being watched. It's weird and familiar. I'm in a major airport, surrounded by thousands of people but essentially all alone. Moving slower, I look around again but don't notice anything or even anyone of interest. I try to shrug it off and tell myself, *Calm down, El. You're giving yourself the heebie-jeebies!* I turn back toward the baggage claim and continue on my way.

JAMES

James Russell has a second to jump behind a display rack as he trails after Ellen. She whips around and looks intently behind her and almost catches him. *Girl must have eyes in the back of her head*. He doesn't know if he should approach her or if he will learn more by simply observing for the moment. Will she meet someone? What's she up to? Deciding to act, James moves up on Ellen as she approaches the carousel where her baggage will come out. She stops and bending slightly over looks up the turnstiles as if the act of wanting it to move will actually make it move. Standing straight, she bounces a bit on the balls of her feet and looks left and right and then she seems to sense the large presence behind her. She looks over her shoulder and up into James Russell's eyes.

ELLEN

"Holy Shit!" I utter, as I step back I almost fall into the carousel. The only thing that stops me from sitting on it is James reaching out and grabbing me around the waist. He lifts me up and into him and sets me back on my feet, then he takes a step back.

"Hello, Ellen."

"What the hell are you doing here?" I exclaim. "This is Italy! What are you doing here?" I ask again. I look around like maybe I'm somewhere I don't think or don't know. With a wrinkle of my brow I ask, "Don't you work?"

"Of course I work. Even cops take vacations. You left without allowing us to finish our conversation," he says, like it's the most natural thing imaginable to have followed me halfway around the world.

Heedless of other people and making a scene, I push through him and turn on him, "What are you, some kind of psycho? This is taking stalking to a whole 'nother realm, James!"

"I'm not stalking you, Ellen. I have questions about this situation and I have to admit it's driving me a bit crazy." He gives me a small embarrassed smile. "I know there's a bigger story here and..." He walks away from me and then spins back. He paces closer and adds, "Ok...and I want to be part of it. I know this is a big deal, I can feel it. I want to know everything and I want to help you, be your partner, if you will."

I don't say anything. This is either the worst thing that could happen, or the best. I already know I like James Russell — I mean LIKE James Russell. It sure would make this trip more interesting to have him around and to have another person to bounce ideas off can't be bad. I mean, he's a cop for Christ's sake, he can certainly handle himself, and I'm sure he'll come in handy.

I lean into him and give a little smile. "Is that the only luggage you have? We have plans to make."

8

After we retrieve our luggage, we head for the exit. I've made reservations at a local hotel, so the plan is to go to my hotel, order food, clean up and discuss the situation. I'm not having second thoughts. I actually feel better having James with me, but I don't want to tell him everything right away. My instincts continue to ding me in the head and tell me to keep my secrets to myself for a bit longer.

At the hotel, I check in and James gets another room on the same floor. We decide to meet back in an hour and order room service so we'll have privacy to discuss our next step. "I guess you might as well come back here in an hour. It really doesn't matter which room we eat in, right?"

He nods. "I'll see you in an hour then."

Fifty minutes later, I'm showered and dressed in fresh clothes. My hotel room is nice. It's modest but clean, with a queen bed and plenty of light from a large window that overlooks a busy street. I expect James at any moment.

When he arrives, we order room service and begin to discuss the situation that brought us to Italy. I want to keep all my information very general — I'm here in search of something I have some information on and don't know exactly how I'm going to locate it, what it is or what I'll be doing with it when and if I find it.

"I don't understand, Ellen. You came all this way with so little information? Where are you going to start? Where will you look? What are you looking for?"

My head hurts as I try to come up with a plausible explanation without giving him too much information. "I don't know where I was going to start. My plan was to work that out when I arrived."

"Well, now you've arrived. What facts do you have? Let me know and I'll help you with a plan."

I pace to the door and stand with my back to him thinking frantically. I don't know why I want to keep the information I got from Joe Bell to myself. It feels special to be just mine. Once I share it, I'm afraid the glow and mystery will dim. I want James with me; I look forward to getting to know him better, but this puzzle is mine.

"What aren't you telling me, Ellen?"

I decide to avoid any mention of "Poppy Flowers".

"I received a key from Joe Bell. I'm interested in what it may open…"

"Joe Bell? How and when?"

"It's complicated, James, but it's the reason I've come to Naples. I believe the key belongs here and when used, it'll help me continue with my search for an item. I don't know what it is, but I have reason to believe it's rare and valuable."

"What reason? You must have more information than what you're giving me. How do you expect me to help you with only half the facts?"

"Ok, Sergeant Friday," I mumble under my breath.

"Ellen…"

I glance at him and see he has this hyper-patient expression on his face. It makes me feel even more infantile and silly to be withholding information.

I want to bang my head against the wall; or maybe I'll bang Detective Russell — James' head! *Arghhh, men!* He keeps picking at me, no — interrogating me, with questions.

"Ellen. You need to let me in on what you know."

What a cop! When I still don't give him any new answers he adopts this suffering, condescending look that tells me he knows something more is up. He wants to know everything and isn't going to give up. I want to trust him.

"Okay," I say and James looks up at me expectantly from the seat he's taken. "I have some additional information and I'm going to take a huge leap of faith and share it with you and trust you'll work with me."

James shifts and gives me a five hundred watt smile. "Finally," he says with a sigh. I feel an explosion in my head and have to blink and sit myself down. Wow! If I thought he was attractive before, when he looks at me like that and smiles I can't even breathe.

"So Ellen," he says. "Talk to me. Let me help you."

I explain what he's missed the last couple of days and he sits quietly and listens. "I don't know if the robbery at my apartment is tied to all of this or not. It might just be a coincidence; although I realize now, as I cleaned my apartment, I couldn't locate the hand mirror I bought from Mr. Bell."

"Can I see the items you got from him?" he asks.

Digging in my bag, I pull out an envelope that holds the original note and the key from the music box. With a hesitant step, I walk toward him. I take a deep breath and hold out the envelope. James takes it and pulls out the two items. He reads the note over twice and looks long and hard at the key.

"Well?" I say. "What do you think? Do you think the painting might be in whatever this key opens up? I thought Joe Bell sounded like he might be Italian. Do you think he used to live here?"

James shrugs, "I'm not sure what's going on with Joe Bell's history.

Boyd and I discovered this Joe Bell didn't exist more than four years ago."

"What?" I ask incredulously. I take a step toward him and demand, "And when were you going to tell me that?"

"Give and take, Little El. Give and take." He touches my face gently. I freeze at the contact of his fingertips; even my breath stops. *Wow, he sure does pack a punch!* I lean my head into his hand. For a moment he stills and then he smiles that smile again. I smile back.

"So, what are your thoughts? Where are you going from here?" James asks.

Reluctantly, I step back and begin to pace again. With my hands on my hips, I walk with my head down, thinking out loud. "We need to find someone who can link the image on the key with a location. Then maybe the number on the other side will identify a box or something it opens." I raise my eyebrows at him. "You think?"

"I think that's as good a plan as any — and better than some. We should get some rest and begin fresh in the morning." James opens the door and turns back to me, "Goodnight, Ellen." He steps into the hallway pulling the door shut.

After he's gone, *most abruptly*, I lie on the hotel bed and try to get some rest but sleep won't come easily. I consider the last couple days. Who would want Mr. Bell dead? Who was Joe Bell? What's his history? Who has the "Poppy Flowers"? Is MY life in danger? What will we find as we continued our search? I think about James Russell. As my mind floats, I fall asleep....

MARIA 2011

Joseph Cabana looks at his sister with disbelief. "Why do you ask this of me? Do you WANT me to go away?"

"Really, Joseph," Maria coaxes, "it's not such a big deal. You know I can't go. You're the only one who can find Angelo. Without you, who will I turn to?" She squeezes out a tear and turns large pleading eyes to her big brother.

Joseph and Maria share many of the same physical traits, traits that on Maria are true gifts, but on Joseph make him look effeminate and weak. Their smaller stature and fine features draw people to Maria like moths to a flame, but the same traits push people away from Joseph. Even their own father prefers Maria to his elder son. But Maria knows Joseph loves her and he'll do anything for her — even this, even leave his home, travel to different lands, and change his name... all to find the man she loves.

"*Si, La Sorella Bella*. I'll hunt down your man and bring him home — I swear it."

With satisfaction Maria beams a glowing smile. "I know you won't fail me *IL fratello*. You are always my champion!"

Joseph preens like he is ten feet tall as Maria describes her plan to find Angelo. Soon after Angelo left he sent Maria a postcard with a gift of a music box. She'd been so excited to receive something from him; she didn't think he'd contact her again. She opened the package and looked at the little music box with...well? With confusion. How could he send her something so provincial? What is she, a farmer's wife? Maria is a beloved only daughter of a powerful and wealthy man — she entertains heads of state and leaders of the underworld alike. She routinely receives gifts of jewels, cars and clothing. One man, in an attempt to woo her, gave her a race horse. She looks at the small wooden box with distaste and doesn't even remove it from the package. *Maybe Angelo wasn't the man for her*, she thinks. She'll do what is necessary to get him back and then it will be HER who ends their relationship, not the other way around. One good thing about the card and package is it tells Maria where to send Joseph. Naples, Mount Vesuvius. That's where the gift comes from. The note, card and music box means less than nothing to her but they may come in handy for Joseph while he searches for Angelo, so she will send it with him. She decides to put the original note in the hiding spot of her mirror and send it with Joseph. If need be, it'll be proof that she sent Joseph and she wants him back.

To eliminate any hint of this coming back on the family, Joseph will change his name. Through family connections, Maria has already purchased new papers for him — an ID and plane tickets. Maria never had any doubts about Joseph's decision to help her.

As Joe Bell, Joseph will leave Venice for Naples to take up the trail to find Angelo. He'll have adequate money for an extended stay and additional travel, although Maria is confident he'll find Angelo quickly. Soon! Soon she'll have her Angelo back! Then he'll learn his lesson. No man leaves Maria unless it's her idea!

9

ELLEN

Early the next morning I'm up, showered and ready to go when James knocks at my hotel room. I'm almost running to the door with excitement at seeing him again. I peek through the peep hole and open the door with a smile.

"Good morning, Sunshine," he says with an answering grin. "Did you miss me?"

I don't answer him. I don't know what to say that isn't too telling. I step back into the room, opening the door wide and James walks in. He turns to me as I close the door. "Ready to go?" At my nod, he adds, "how about some breakfast. There are a couple of small cafes down the street, then we can start asking around about the key."

"I had a thought," I say. "I took a picture of the key with my phone and emailed it to my account. Let's stop in the computer center downstairs and make some blown-up pictures of the key. That way it'll be easier to see and the key will remain safe."

"Now you're thinking like a cop!"

Little did I know we weren't the only ones in Naples on the hunt for the "Poppy Flowers". Would I have changed my plans if I knew?

MARCO

When the couple exits the hotel, Marco and the three men with him notice. They've waited at a café down the street for the pair to move. If one watched the men intently, they would notice the tightening of their hands on their cups, the narrowing of their eyes and the very small lapse in conversation. But no one watches and the moment passes. Three of the men go back to an argument over the soccer game on the radio, and the remaining man stands apart.

Marco has never been a joiner, a talker. He doesn't like people and usually works alone, but the Lady asked him to work with the other men for this assignment and since he'll do anything for her, he'll work with the men — but he doesn't like it. Their conversations grate on his ears and their opinions and frivolous behaviors make him want to put a bullet in their three little heads. He smiles a secret smile to himself and thinks, perhaps when this is all over, he'll ask the Lady if he can help these three men move on to their next lives. He knows she likes to make him happy and if he was a betting man, he'd bet she'll let him do whatever he wants to the three behind him. Marco loves the Lady. She's his savior and if she asks anything of him, he will give it.

MARCO 2011

The fighter stands in the cage and can't help but notice when the woman walks into the basement. He's bloody, sweaty and exhausted from his last bout but even from across the room he can smell her fresh scent, like a breeze blown in from a garden. If he knew flowers, he'd know she smells of gardenias. His breath is heavy due to his recent contest, but he draws in extra-long and tries to hold it to make her scent a part of him.

She's different from any of the other women present, classier. Her clothing and jewelry is a finer quality than he's used to seeing and just the way she moves he can tell she's never been somewhere like this underground fight club. He's the best fighter in the network and does it for the money and the thrill of beating a man to death; and it's all he knows. Marco has fought since he was too big for the men to want in other ways and since he was big enough to put on a good show and earn a few dollars. As he grew older and bigger and meaner, he became the one to beat. He's a valuable commodity for the man who owns him.

That man stops in front of him now and pulls the garden woman with him by the arm. She's not only reluctant to be here, but to get this close to him — the beast in the cage.

"Look at him!" the man yells. "Like a prize stallion! He'll make me a fortune!"

Elevated inside the cage, Marco looks down at the man who, for now, owns him — life and limb. The woman stands next to him. She cringes, with her head down between her shoulders. The man wraps a big hairy arm around her and pulls her to the bars.

"Look! Look at him, Maria!" He urges her up close to Marco as he stands there silently and looks down at her. At his urging, she tips her head hesitantly up and looks him in the eye.

His breath catches in his lungs; Marco can't move. She's beautiful — like a Madonna. Now that he can see her face, he realizes she's aglow from the inside. What is she? An angel come down to earth? The Virgin Mother? How can the man dare to dishonor her with his crassness, his brutality? Marco and the woman stare at each other and neither of them draw a breath — each sees their own salvation.

*****

Maria enters the fight area with disgust and trepidation. She can't believe her father will give her to this man, sell her really, for a business deal. Naturally, they are to wed, but she'll still be a slave, a breed mare for an old, sweaty, disgusting man. How is she to survive a life with a man who thinks human cock fighting is something you take a well-bred woman to see, especially the woman you are to marry.

They enter the room and Carlos drags her with him toward the cage. The smell of the place is confined and hot, ripe with human rot, close to making her gag. People are jammed in, yelling out bets and taunts. They're all dirty and smelly — even the women, who not only smell like they haven't bathed in their lives, but like they've heaped cheap perfume on top of that. Maria loves her personal perfume — *Tuvache Jungle Gardenia*. It's classy and expensive, like her. How these heathens can exist, she doesn't know. As Carlos pulls her toward the cage he shouts about his purchase of this fighter and how he'll make him money. The one thing Carlos has is money. That's the reason her father deemed him worthy of his time and now his daughter, that and the fact her beauty is marred by her scar. Carlos wraps his meaty arm around her and she cringes into herself. His smell is so offensive she has to hold her breath or she'll be physically ill all over the floor - not that anyone will notice her addition of filth, not in this place. In an attempt to make Carlos back away and halt his yelling, Maria looks at the fighter on the platform. Her body freezes and her breath catches as she looks him in the eye. This is a killer — she can see the fierceness in him. How did he come to be owned by another? He stares at her as if she can save him from drowning. She nods her head slightly at him and acknowledges his need and her ability to turn it into what she wants.

Carlos and Maria leave the basement together and walk toward his limo. He's talking loudly and gesturing, keyed up from the fight, the blood and death and especially the money he's won. After she slides into his vehicle, Maria squeezes herself against the far door.

The door locks click and she's shocked to hear Carlos lewdly say to his driver, "Head to the estate first. Maria can go home to daddy later. I want to sample what I'm paying for."

"Wait, Carlos!" she shouts with panic from the backseat. "My father will be angry. He's very religious; there's protocol to this arrangement." At this point Maria will say anything to be released from this car.

Carlos laughs cruelly and climbs into the back with her. He pulls the door shut with a slam. "Your father isn't such a big man, you know.

I'll do as I want. And right now, I want a taste of my new purchase."

Maria's mind scrambles as she tries to discover a way she can get out of this. Carlos slides across the seat toward her. He grabs her leg and digs his fingers in. He pulls her across the leather, causing her to scream in fear at the lust in his eyes and the pain in the grip on her thigh. Suddenly, from outside there's a sound — a crunch and something falls against the car, shaking it. Both Maria and Carlos freeze and look toward the door, the assault on Maria momentarily forgotten.

"Who's there?" Carlos calls out. "Dante? What are you doing?"

Maria hears the panicky sound of their breath in the car and her own heartbeat, but other than that there's complete silence. Carlos screws up his courage, opens the door and steps out into the night. Abruptly, he's yanked away and the door is slammed shut.

Maria is terrified! Her eyes are open so wide they bulge and her breath comes in short little pants. What's happening? Is she going to die? From outside the car she hears muffled sounds, like a bat hitting a sack of grain over and over. She's hyper-sensitive to every nuance of the sounds outside, but can't place what's happening. Then silence; silence so deep. Maria strains to hear something, anything. Just as she thinks she's going to have to try the car door, it opens. The light from the overhead spills out onto the street which is wet with something. What's on the street? Why is it so dark? She refuses to acknowledge the unique, coppery scent. Her breath comes in short spurts and she's light-headed. She takes a deep breath and then another to calm herself. She steps out of the vehicle and moves from the door. A few feet away is a lone man on his knees. Where is Carlos? Where is his driver? She glances around and realizes she is completely alone with the man. As she walks to him, he tips up his head and she recognizes the face of the fighter from the basement arena.

"Lady," he says. "I am yours."

The sound of the men's boisterous laughing behind him returns

Marco's thoughts from the past to his current situation. *Yes, yes, he thinks with satisfaction. When this job is done, the Lady will give those three to me.*

10

ELLEN

James and I know it'll be faster to separate and ask around about the key but we aren't completely confident in the area and so decide to stay together. We have a map of the city and for this first day we've marked off a span of approximately five square miles. If we hit every few businesses, we can cover the area and perhaps get lucky and find someone who recognizes the image on the key, who can direct us to the right location.

Naples is a beautiful city, with fresh sea air and museums around every corner. I have trouble keeping my thoughts centered on the search for a link to the key with all the artwork and history before my eyes. I feel like a child in a candy shop who's told I can't eat anything. I know I'm pouting, but it's so unfair to be in this amazing city and to be limited to a plan that doesn't include simple sightseeing.

About two hours in I tell myself I'm going to speak with James about an allotment of time for personal adventuring. I really can't take it, no matter how hard I try. The statues, museums, churches, monasteries...I feel like I'm going to have to be sedated if I can't take time and spend it in admiration and learning about Naples.

Towards evening James and I find a café to sit and eat.

"What do you think?" I ask James. "It's like the key and the image are completely foreign to this area. If I get one more blank look I may scream."

"It has been disappointing." He gives a sigh. "Tomorrow we'll try again. Maybe we'll get lucky."

Here's my opening, I think.

"James," I look down at my hands. Like a high school girl, I'm worried about his reaction. Maybe it's my own guilt talking, like I'm not taking our quest seriously. This puzzle has been mine but now that we're a team I want to carry my weight. "I'd like to spend some time sightseeing while we're in Naples." I glance up to try and gauge his reaction and then rush on. "I realize we're here for a reason and we need to find something that leads to the key, but truthfully, I just can't take it. I know I'll be more focused if I take an hour or two to enjoy the other sights." Getting it out I give a sigh of relief.

James smiles a little and shakes his head. "Ellen, I'm just a tagalong. This is my first break from work in years and I'm enjoying it. If you want to see other things, then I think we should. So far your instincts have been right on track." He reaches across the table and touches my hand. "Let's discuss a less rigid plan for tomorrow, okay?"

A brilliant smile crosses my face at his words and I gush, "Wonderful! I'd love to see some churches and perhaps the catacombs! The catacombs are Paleo-Christian burial sites and there are many…."

11

As the next day progresses there's a different feel to our moods. We'll spend part of the day asking around about the key, but part of it'll be spent on a tour of a church — the *Cathedral of San Gennaro* is the first one I select, and *Catacombe di San Gennaro*. James has an indulgent smile but he appears to enjoy the change. About three hours into our day we've exhausted the businesses to show the picture of the key to and we head to the church and catacombs. As we walk down the street laughing a man bumps into us, forcing us apart and knocking me into the wall of a building.

"Hey!" James yells as he reaches out to steady me.

"*A fanabla!*" the man yells back, making a rude gesture at us.

"Pardon me?!" James shouts, and he heads for the man.

"*Fanculo Voi!*"

I grab his arm. "James…James, let it go. Let's have a nice day. You can't help that some people are rude. I'm fine." I've never seen him like this, so angry, so quickly. James stops and looks down at me with a scowl, he's obviously undecided. I take his arm, turn him down the street and begin to walk; gently I pull him with me. He allows himself to be led but turns his head and watches the man enter a door to what appears to be an above street apartment.

When we get to the church, I stop before I ascend the stone stairs.

I look at the church façade, heave a big sigh and say, "Oh, James. Don't you think this is simply beautiful?"

"Yes, beautiful."

I realize he's staring at me with an appreciative look. I smile brightly and give him a little push. "No, silly! The church! It's amazing and the history is staggering! Let's go," I say and run up the stairs.

I am in heaven! In the church we see frescoes and altarpieces and other great works of art. We hear the legend of the 'Miracle of the Blood' which pertains to a vial containing the blood of Saint Januarius which is brought out twice a year when the dried blood usually liquefies. Legend states that if the blood fails to liquefy, disaster will befall Naples.

When the tour of the church finishes we head to the catacombs. Both of us are tired, but want to finish our plans for the day before we stop to get a bite to eat. As we tour the catacombs, it's obvious James is enjoying himself. He asks questions and is interested. The catacombs are a set of underground burial sites in the northern part of the city. In the catacombs are more frescoes that depict the people buried there. As we come out of the catacombs, I stop James, laughing. "I really have to eat something or I'm going to fall over!"

James takes my hand and we walk until we find a quaint café with street seating, where we enjoy lunch.

On the walk back to our hotel we wander up and down some side streets. I think I hear the splash of water. Naples is full of fountains and they're all big and beautiful and a favorite of mine.

"James! Do you hear the water? Let's look for the fountain."

With a nod, he allows me to drag him by the hand down the next street. As we come out on the sidewalk, the street we're on opens into an intersection surrounded with large buildings. In front of one of the buildings, in an atrium setting, is a large beautiful fountain. I walk closer, and suddenly stop. With a start I place my fingers to my temple. The Buzz is deafening. "It's a mermaid," I whisper.

Could this be the link to the key? Is this the mermaid we've looked for?

James looks intently at the fountain and walks closer. I'm right, it is a mermaid and she's surrounded by animals — what looks to be a lion, dolphin, horse and turtle. The garden where the fountain is located is almost deserted. Only a couple of people walk by. As James leaves the nearby buildings and approaches the fountain, a breeze off the ocean catches him and ruffles his hair. He stops and glances back at me.

"Ellen?" he asks. "Are you coming? Let's take a closer look."

I'm still studying the fountain from the street, but I drop my hands and I walk towards him. I wonder. What will we find?

I look up to see the face of the mermaid. The fountain must be almost fifteen feet tall and it's surrounded by a moat of water. The mermaid and animals rest on a stone base that's coarsely built; fine sprays of water jet out around it. The mermaid is on her knees with a clam shell in one hand and the other raised above her. I walk around the fountain on the outside of the moat while James trails me. I look at it from all sides. *It really is quite beautiful*. Marble. I pull the key out of my pants pocket and strain to look at it in the fading light. With a burst of inspiration, I jump up to the walkway on the outside of the moat. I replace the key in my pocket and reach into my bag to pull out my flashlight. I step down into the water and click on my light.

"Ellen, be careful," I hear James softly caution me.

With an absent nod, I begin to walk around the fountain through the knee deep water, splashing gently. My boots and pants becoming quickly saturated. James tracks me on the outside of the base and watches my every move.

Partway around the fountain, under the lion, I stop the forward motion of my light and backtrack. Something catches my eye and that old familiar feeling is pinging. The top of my head tingles like drops of water are running down it and my fingers are numb. Something is there. A little area, kind of a gap in the stone of the base. I lean forward, into and past the spray of water. I get close with my light and squint at the area. The beam reflects on something inside: like a metal mechanism. A key lock? I slide my hand into my pocket and again pull out the mermaid key. With a tight hold on it, I slide my fingers with the key into the stone. As I push forward about two inches I can't see my fingers and I'm afraid I'm going to lose the key when suddenly, it stops moving and I hear a barely audible click.

When I pull my fingers and the key out of the base, it moves with me. *Holy Crap!* I think. I turn and give James a look and put the key in my pocket. I pull the movable piece of the base open. Inside, safe and dry is an envelope. It looks to be leather or some other material. As I grasp it, the texture and softness imprint in my mind. I take the envelope from the cubby hole and shine my light in to verify there is nothing else. I push the piece back into the base and put the package inside my shirt under my jacket. Standing straight, I head toward James. I slosh through the water to the edge and reach to take his offered hand. He's on the walkway and pulls me up next to him.

"Let's get out of here," I say as I look up at him with eyes that won't quite focus.

"Come on," he agrees. He hops off the walkway and reaches up to grasp me under my arms and lifts me down. As we head up the street, I shiver with cold and reaction to all that's happened. I glance up at James, who has his arm around me as we hurry along the street and I let him direct me as he will. At the fountain I felt led, drawn to do what was necessary to find the items. Now I feel like a rag doll, as if I've blown a lobe out of my brain; I'm foggy…

James stares down at me with concern and he moves a little faster. We come around a corner and I see our hotel in front of me as it comes closer and closer. Soon James has me in the elevator and then at the door of my room. He releases me and takes my bag. Without asking, he begins to rummage in it but I don't have the energy to protest. He pulls out my card key and opens the door. He moves me inside and says, "Why don't you put the things you found on the table — I promise I won't touch them — and get into a hot shower? When you're done, we'll look at it together."

I nod to him and glance at the bathroom but don't move. The cold water trickles down my shins, pooling in my socks and boots. *Wow* I think. *I can't seem to get my body to obey my head.*

James steps to me and opens my jacket. He reaches under my shirt and removes the envelope. Catching my eye, he walks to the table, deliberately sets the envelope down and steps back from it. He turns me toward the bathroom, giving me a little push. I walk into the bathroom, closing the door behind me. I turn on the water, strip and get in. The water feels amazing and with its warmth comes clarity. Hurrying now, I finish and when dry, wrap my hair in a towel and my body in a hotel robe. I open the door to find James sitting on the bed looking across the room at the items on the table. When he hears me, he glances my way and raises his eyebrows.

"Wow, huh?" he says with understated accuracy.

I nod and walk to the table to pick up the envelope, turn and bring it to the bed. I climb on the bed, sit cross-legged and place the envelope between us. James spins around and faces me as he crosses his arms and waits.

Seeing the envelope in the bright light of the room, I realize it's a leather-like fabric, dark brown with texture. The color stands out starkly against the off-white bed spread. I remember, when I took it from the fountain it was heavy and something shifted in it; this now happens again. I pull the envelope toward me and unhook the seal. Twine is wrapped around the edges to keep the packet securely closed. I remove the contents, setting the empty envelope to the side. The items move and a grey stone falls out. It looks like a wagon wheel with five spokes. It's smooth and fits in the palm of my hand. I turn it over and hold it up to get a better look. There're no marks or writing on it; it's worn by time. I give James a one-sided shrug and hand it to him. He gingerly takes the wheel. He turns it this way and that, hefts it as though he's checking the weight. I wait for something to happen or for him to have some insight into what it is. We're together in our confusion, however, and he sets it on the bed. I pick up a sheet folded in half. After I open it, I read aloud to James:

My Dearest Maria:

I knew you would be worthy, My Love. It pleases me you have come this far and just this knowledge helps me continue. I feel you in my veins and it keeps me grounded when the 'Poppies' call to me, as they do incessantly. I will continue to strive for an answer – or I will simply be consumed. We are like two parts of a whole, ripped apart. Will we be together again?

Either way, you are in my heart.

Angelo

"So Angelo hopes Maria will find him, or at least follow him?" James asks.

"It appears so. I wonder what he means by being 'worthy'. He's used that term a couple times."

James shakes his head and gives a little shrug. "What else is there?"

I separate the remaining papers and pull out one that looks and feels different. Its papyrus and has an etching on it. I'm reminded of a pencil transfer from a gravestone but this one has Egyptian hieroglyphics on it. I show it to James and with a lift of my eyebrows say, "Too bad we can't read hieroglyphics. You can't, can you?"

James shakes his head. "Sadly, no."

There are three images on the papyrus paper. One looks like a figure of a seated man in profile, one a triangle with a base and one a tower. All the figures are to one side of the paper and the other side is blank.

What remains is a card with a poem:

In Pharaoh's land, stone twins were born,

Chiseled and shaped, their messages worn.

Past eons and ages, they stood silent guard,

Their watch continuous, their duty unmarred.

With a gift of a king, the twins were torn,

Never reunited, their new lands adorn.

Their vigil now lone, one in sand and one in light,

Obelisks parted, stand tall with their might.

I read the card again, out loud, in an attempt to understand. James holds out his hand. "Can I see it?"

"Of course," I hand it to him. "So Pharaoh's land would be Egypt, right? And Obelisks are stone towers." I feel my eyes round for a moment and my breath catch. "Oh wow," I whisper.

James looks from the card and asks, "What? Did you think of something?"

"Oh my goodness! I may already have a piece to this puzzle." I hurry to my bags. Reaching in, I dig to the bottom and pull out the envelope that contains the items I retrieved from Joe Bell's garage. "How could I have forgotten about this stuff? It seems like eons ago when I was there." I come back to the bed and climb on. I open the envelope to take out the papers, shuffling through them until I come across a postcard with a courtyard. In the middle of the courtyard is an Egyptian obelisk. "Here!" I exclaim and hand the card to James.

"Where's this stuff from?" he asks, indicating the packet in my hand.

"Joe Bell's garage."

"What? What do you mean 'Joe Bell's garage'?"

"It's a long story and I'll tell you all about it, but I received an email from Joe Bell after he was already dead and it led me to some stuff in his garage. I went back, found it and took it."

"From an active crime scene? Where a murder was committed?" James has an incredulous expression.

"Yes. And don't be such a cop. It happened and I have the stuff and nothing can change that. Look at the card!"

James gives me a long look of disapproval. "I want to see what else you have in there."

"Yes, yes...we'll go through it. What do you think of the card?"

James studies the card. It's a photo of a stone tower surrounded by buildings — beautiful, European-style buildings. He turns it over, looking at the backside.

Learning is a *Journey*,

It begins as flowers bud,

A *Craft* is complete with autumn.

James reads it out loud. "Do you know what it means?" he asks.

"No, not yet."

"*l Aiguille de Cleopatre*?" he reads.

"Yes! And I know exactly what that is! Maybe they have to do with each other." I'm about to bounce off the walls! I get up and pace around the room. "There's an Egyptian Obelisk in the middle of Paris! It was a gift, just like in the poem, from the ruler of Egypt to the King of France in the 1800s. They literally picked it up and moved it to France. That must be what the poem talks about! 'One in sand and one in light'. Paris is the City of Light. *l Aiguille de Cleopatre* is Cleopatra's Needle. That's what the obelisk is called. I think he's directing Maria to Paris — I think that's where we need to go. The twins were divided as he and Maria are divided."

James nods his head. He picks up the stone wheel. "Do you have any ideas about what this is? What it's used for?"

"I don't but it seems very old and it may have some use with the obelisk. What do you think? Do you agree? Paris?"

"Yes. I think all of the clues definitely point that way. And maybe we'll figure out the other part, the short poem, when we get there. Let's go."

"I'll get on line and get us a flight."

"Before you do that, let's hear about Joe Bell's garage..."

After I share my story of the night at Joe Bell's garage, I check on flights and book us on AirFrance. It's a quick hop from Naples to Charles de Gaulle National Airport in Paris. We'll leave the next day, late morning.

"I feel funny asking this, James, but I'm feeling kind of freaked out. Would you stay here tonight? I'm happy to take the couch."

"Of course I don't mind. And I'll take the couch. I've slept in worse places," he adds with a wink. "Let me run to my room and get some things. I'll be right back."

After James goes to his room, I get myself ready for bed — PJs on, teeth brushed, face washed...with my head in a spin I wait for James to come back. I find spare blankets and a pillow which I place on the couch. Tomorrow we'll continue on this quest to track Angelo and find "Poppy Flowers". This latest development happened so quickly and unexpectedly. I'm still attempting to wrap my head around it.

When there's a soft knock on the door, I let James in. He has a small bag and drops it near the couch. He turns and looks at me. I feel a little nervous and give him a small smile. "Guess I'll get some sleep, then," I say.

He nods at me. "I can turn out the light."

I climb into bed and pulling the blankets up to my chin, I turn my back to him and try to relax. I really like James Russell and I'm sure I'm correct that he returns my feelings. I'm not an innocent little girl, but it isn't in my nature to jump into a relationship too quickly and although due to circumstances this relationship has been propelled into an intimacy very quickly, I don't have the guts to take the next step without more input from him — no matter how much I'd like to.

James comes out of the bathroom and shuts off the light, then makes his way through the darkness to the couch. As I lay in the quiet and dark, I say, "James?"

"Um?"

"Tell me something about yourself. Your family or something?"

"Well? There's not much to tell."

"Aw, come on," I prompt. "There must be something you can tell me."

"Well? I had kind of a rough start in life. My mother was very young when I was born and couldn't care for me, so I ended up in the foster care system. I lived with different people — all good people, for the first part of my life. When I was a bit older, I was adopted by a nice couple. They're the only family I have and I refer to them as my mother and father."

As he speaks it's with matter-of-factness and very little emotion. I'm sure there's a lot of pain and history hidden he isn't letting on. "So your birth mother isn't in your life at all?"

"She died when I was young. We didn't have much of a relationship. I really didn't know her."

"I'm sorry, James." When he doesn't answer I add, "I'm glad you're spending your time here with me."

"I'm glad to be with you too, Ellen."

I don't even realize I've fallen asleep until I partially awaken in the middle of the night. The sound of the hotel door as it closes quietly rouses me and I mutter, "James? Is that you?"

"Shhh," he answers. "It's just me. Go back to sleep; everything's ok."

I sigh, reassured, and drift back to sleep.

12

At the airport the next day as we wait in the line for security, I robotically watch the monitors run the local news until one story in particular catches my eye. "Look, James," I say. "There was a murder right by where we stayed."

With a look of surprise, James watches the news story. "Good thing we're leaving, huh? I guess all countries have some of the same problems."

Just then, the line for security begins to move and we drop the subject.

Other flights are emptying as we move toward our gate and as is typical with a large airport there are people everywhere. The sound is a constant hum that reminds me of a swarm of bees interspersed with announcements in multiple languages. Suddenly I hear a woman shout, "Why James Russell! What are you doing here?"

I watch as James smiles down at a petite, blonde woman. Honestly, a Barbie doll of a woman.

Really? I think sarcastically. *Can you spell AUGMENTATION?* I know it isn't fair and this blonde bombshell is probably a very nice person, but REALLY?

I roll my eyes and feel my temper heat as James leans down to kiss the woman on the cheek.

"Meredith. It's wonderful to see you," he says. "I assume you're on one of your journeys?"

Meredith laughs and lays a hand on his arm. She flips her hair and leans in to whisper, "Oh, you know me! I love to jet set all over."

James chuckles and turns to me, placing a hand on my shoulder to draw me near. His touch surprises me and seems to heat throughout my arm. "Meredith, I'd like you to meet my friend, Ellen."

Just as Meredith says, "Friend?" I think *"Friend?"* with an arched eyebrow. I regain my composure, smile and nod at Meredith. "Nice to meet you," I say.

"We're just heading out and need to make our gate, but it's wonderful to see you. I'll tell my mother I saw you and you said hello," he says.

"Of course, of course. Give my best to her and your father, please. Nice to meet you, Ellen," she says with a forced smile as she turns and walks into the crowd.

After finding our gate, James and I sit in a couple open seats. "Meredith seemed nice," I volunteer.

James turns to look at me, but doesn't say anything. He just watches me.

"Close friend of yours?" I ask.

He smiles that slow devastating smile and doesn't give me an answer. I feel my eyes narrow. *Isn't he going to say anything?* I grab a magazine from my bag and leaf through it. James sits back in his chair and seems to be people watching. I know I should let it go, I have no hold on him; I barely know him, right? But the image of the little Barbie with the boobies and blonde hair pokes my temper.

I slap the magazine down on my lap and turn toward him. James watches me and appears to be waiting. "So?" I say, but he doesn't volunteer anything. *Damn him.*

"Ok. So Meredith is very pretty. All little and blonde and stuff. Have you known her for a long time?"

"Ellen," James sits straight and leans toward me. "I do like you jealous." Just as my brain registers his comment and I'm beginning to get a head of temper he says, "Meredith is a family friend. She's done some charity work with my mother and I've known her for years." He waits a beat and adds, "But she's not my type."

Now I feel sheepish and with a slight blush I ask, "No?"

"No," he says. I've always preferred a woman who looks like a woman, one who's my equal in every way." As he leans forward, he comes within an inch or two of me, so we're nose to nose, "and I prefer brunettes." He closes the distance between us to touch his lips to mine. I feel this wonderful heat and at the same time I shiver as my eyes drift shut. I can still hear the hum of background noise from the people but find my whole being is focused on this one area where we touch. James opens his mouth a bit and touches his tongue to my lips, inviting me to respond. Gladly, I open my mouth and lean into him. The kiss is gentle and teasing and perfect. A moment later I pull away reluctantly and look into his eyes. "Okay?" he says.

"Okay." I answer.

When we board our airplane there's plenty of room and this promises to be a nice flight. We get to our row and James moves to give me the window seat, which is nice since I love to look outside. Our conversation is a bit stilted as everyone boards but soon we take off. The flight's a short one and I relax more and more with James and it seems he's also relaxing with me. I find myself captivated by this man. After we're served a snack and drink, feeling sleepy I lay my head on James' shoulder. He reaches over, takes my hand in his and places it down on his thigh. Gently he holds it there, caressing my fingers and relaxing into his chair. His hand moves over mine, rhythmic and soothing and soon I fall asleep.

*****

The sound of the landing gear, as they lock into place, wakes me. Yawning, I move and shift into James.

"Hello Sleepy Head," he says softly against my hair.

Ah, I think. This man has so easily wormed his way into my head and heart. Should I throw up some barriers or just open up and let him in? I rub my face gently on his shoulder as I think. I'm thirty-five years old; I've had serious relationships before. I'm not all that innocent and certainly not naïve. It's a bit scary to like him so much so quickly. Maybe I'll be observant and keep the reins on my emotions. *Yes, yes*, I tell myself. *That definitely is the smart thing to do.*

After deplaning in Paris, we walk toward the exit. We haven't discussed what we'll do once we arrive and both of us are quiet, tired from the flight and the last couple days. As we exit the gate, James takes my arm at the elbow and moves me through the mass of departing people to the side of the walkway.

He says, "I have an idea. We're both exhausted from the upheaval of the last week and could use some rest. How about we take a shuttle to a hotel that's close, get some food, shower and sleep and start fresh tomorrow. We'll see what our options are here in Paris and come up with a plan to start investigating the obelisk."

"I think that sounds like a great idea. I could really use some of each."

We decide on a hotel nearby, take the shuttle and soon enter the front doors. It's a lovely hotel with rustic décor and fresh flowers, very welcoming. We walk to the clerk and when he asks about room accommodations I stop with surprise and a jump of nerves. I hadn't thought of this and what it might mean. I look at James and he's looking at me. He simply raises an eyebrow. I guess it's my option to advance this relationship or not — the choice is right in front of me. I make the decision I want. I say, "One room, please."

The room is on the third floor and as we ride up the elevator, emotional fatigue swamps me. I'm dragging. My whole body feels weighed down and my thoughts are sluggish. *Wow, this whole situation has caught up with me fast.* James opens the door and lets me enter first. I drop my bags on the bed. I figure I should be more nervous, but really I'm just too tired.

"Would you like to get some room service?" he asks.

"Yes, I'd love some." I reply with a yawn. "I'm gonna grab a quick shower. Can you get me something with chicken, please? Sandwich or salad."

"Sure. I'll get it ordered, you shower up."

I finish my shower and, opening the door of the bathroom, bring a cloud of steam with me. The room service hasn't arrived, but I figure any minute. James has the TV on low and seems to be zoning out in one of the chairs. When I enter the room, he sits up straight and turns to face me. I blush as he looks me up and down in the terry cloth hotel robe and his eyes shine. When I near him, he takes my hand and pulls me onto his lap. Leaning into me, he snuggles his face into my neck and takes a deep breath. "Ah, you smell wonderful!"

He kisses up my jawline and is moving to my mouth when there's a knock on the door. With my hand on his cheek, I give him a peck on the lips and jump up.

"I'll get it. I'm starved!"

Out of habit, I check the peephole. I glance at myself to ensure I'm decent and open the door. Smiling at the waiter, I gesture him into our room. He moves our meal to the in-room table and when I hand him a tip he says a practiced *"Bon Appetite"* and wheels the cart out the door.

"What do we have?" I ask James.

James ordered me a Tarragon Chicken Salad that has apples and red onions and potatoes with parmesan cheese on the side. I think I'm in heaven. The food is excellent. Between bites I glance at James' ham and cheese sandwich along with some sort of potatoes with onions in them. It smells wonderful.

"Do you have any ideas for tomorrow?" I ask as the food disappears.

"Not right now, but I'm sure some sleep will help our brains come up with something."

After he finishes his sandwich, James says, "I'm going to jump in the shower."

I clean up the dishes and place them outside our hotel room. With the bed open, I lay down to watch TV and listen to the sounds of the shower. I'm more than half asleep when he comes out. I try to rouse myself but he hushes me, drops his towel and slips in the bed. He pulls me into his embrace. His front is along my back and I feel protected and warm as I drift to sleep.

When I awake I'm not sure what time it is but I know we haven't slept long. I smile sleepily as I realize I've woken to his large hand inside my robe on my breast. Shifting a little, I rub my body on James'. His hand begins to caress me, warm and heavy, and I sigh. *This is definitely the way to wake up.* James pushes himself on one elbow and turns me on my back. He grasps my hip and slides me so I am under him, within his arms. I can feel the hard length of him down the side of my body. By the light of the TV I see him — he looks intense and extremely sexy. I no longer have any confusion. I reach to wrap my hand around the nape of his neck and pull him down as I open my heart and body to his welcome embrace.

13

The next morning, we're excited to begin our search and exploration of Paris. I want to jump into the shower first so I bounce out of bed and am voicing my thoughts about where we should start...

"I thought we might go to the location of..." I begin. I've turned to look at James in the bed as I talk and completely lose my train of thought. I smile to myself and finish, "...of the obelisk and look around." He's relaxed with the sheet pulled to his hips and I think there's a definite argument for staying in to investigate the hotel room. *NO!* I tell myself. *We're going to get out and do...and then come back to the room*!

"Do you think that sounds ok?" I ask him.

"I think," says James as he gets up and approaches me, "that you are smart as well as beautiful." He wraps his arms around me and whispers, "Why don't we share that shower?"

*****

Its afternoon before we get started investigating the obelisk — but it was a morning well spent! We stop at the Concierge desk in the hotel lobby and ask, "Do you have information on different sights in Paris?"

"*Oui Mademoiselle.* Alongside the wall next to the door is a rack of tourist information."

"Oh James, I told you. Look at all the wonderful things to do in Paris!" There are pamphlets for the Louvre, the Eiffel Tower, Arc de Triomphe and many, many more. Right in the middle of the other pamphlets sits one with an Egyptian obelisk on it. 'Cleopatra's Needle' is located at the *Place de la Concorde*. I hand James the pamphlet. "So? A taxi ride to the '*Place*'?"

He nods absently as he reads the pamphlet, "Let's grab a taxi out front. This may be it, Ellen," he says. "We might have this solved today."

As we wait outside for the taxi, I tell James about some of my favorite sights in Paris. I place my hand on his arm and tip my head slightly as I ask him, "Have you ever been to Paris?"

"No, how many times have you?" he asks.

"Oh, many times! Paris is one of my favorite cities." I wait a beat and say, "I have an idea."

"What might that be, Ms. Thompson?" he says as he looks down playfully at me. He takes a piece of my hair, wrapping it around his finger.

I lean into him and say, "After we find what we need here, why don't we take a day or two in Paris before we move on? I can show you some of my favorite sites; since we're here — shame to waste it."

He nods and gives me a gentle kiss on the lips. "I would love to see Paris with you."

We arrive at the *Place de la Concorde* and look around in wonder. The day is bright and sunny and a gentle breeze whispers to us with the scent of grass and nature. There are birds calling and the sound of people talking and laughing. As I read from the pamphlet I tell James, "The *Place* is the largest public square in Paris, measuring approximately 20 acres. We need to move to the center of the square where the obelisk is located." Even from where we stand, we can see the spire stretching to the sky, the crown of it reflecting in the bright sunshine. "The top was replaced with a gold inlay. Look how it shines in the light!"

"Let's head over and see what we find," James suggests.

As we near the obelisk, I'm amazed by the sheer size of it. The pamphlet says 75' and 250 metric tons, but that doesn't give a true indication of what it's like to stand in front of something so large. It's brownstone and massive. There's a fence around it so if we're going to get up close it isn't going to be right now — with other tourists and staff about, we'll be stopped immediately. The obelisk stands on a base that has descriptions pertaining to the move from Egypt to Paris and my head barely reaches the juncture. I note all four sides are covered in hieroglyphics, from top to bottom. I'm unable to read them but the information board states they exalt the reign of Ramesses II. *Okay Angelo,* I think. *What now?*

I look at James with a raise of my eyebrows.

"What do you think?" he asks. "I'm not feeling very worthy at this exact moment."

I give a little chuckle. "Let's walk around the obelisk and see if we can find any hieroglyphics that match the ones on the paper."

We separate and each spend time looking at the obelisk. We search for any symbols that look like the three. As I go to the second of four sides, I see what looks like the figure of a man. It's up pretty high and is hard to see so I find James. "Anything?" When he shakes his head in the negative I ask, "Can you look at this part over here? I think there may be a figure but it's up pretty high."

James follows me back to the spot and when I point it out, he squints and nods. "Yep. You're right, it appears to be a figure, and there may be the other symbols there, too. It's up really high though."

"Can you see what else is on the cartouche with it?"

"Um? It's hard to see. If we hadn't been on the lookout for specific images we never would have seen this." James stands with his head back, squinting at the obelisk for a few moments. "No. I can't make it out. I wish there was some way to get up there. Not only for the pictures but the way this has all turned out we can't be sure there isn't another clue."

"You're right." I turn in a complete circle and look closely at the surrounding area. In the distance, near a grove of trees, I spot a service garage. Under my breath I mutter, "I wonder if they have a long ladder in that garage."

James peers at the garage and then at me. "Huh? What are you thinking?"

"If we come back tonight, after the *Place* is vacant, maybe we can climb up and check it out. Finish the etching on the cartouche and look for any other clues."

"Are you trying to get us arrested, Ellen?" James gives me an intense, doubtful look and shakes his head.

"Are you truly planning of giving up? After we've come this far?"

"No." he says. "But I don't want to put us both in a French cell either."

"Well, just for the record, I don't want to be in a French cell. But I will go up that obelisk and look at the cartouche!"

James studies me for a long while and I hold his gaze. At last he says, "Fine. Let's be smart about this, though." He glances at the garage and leans toward me. "Let's wander over and see if we can verify if there is a ladder and if it's long enough; then we'll take it from there."

Pleased, I smile a brilliant smile at him. Taking his arm, I walk toward the garage.

As we approach the service building, a pair of workmen tinker with a vehicle in one stall. We act touristy and wander near the building. While I point out aspects of the history of the area, James covertly studies the interior of the garage. "Well, Ellen, looks like we'll do this your way," James says. "There's an extendable ladder hanging on the wall." He takes my arm and leads me on a route behind the garage away from the open end and the employees. As we get close to the building, he seems to study it.

"Ok," he says. "If you're ready, we can leave. I have all the information we're going to need."

What did he mean by that? What was he thinking?

"Let's find a café, sit and visit." James says.

We sit at a private table drinking coffee and James tells me a bit more about his life. "As I said, I grew up within the foster system for the first part of my childhood. That existence gave me experiences that may come in handy."

I study him with curiosity, but don't say anything.

"I mean," he adds, "I wasn't always a policeman, you know?"

"So what are your thoughts, James?"

Carefully, he lays out the plan he has to get into the garage, get the ladder and check out the cartouche on the obelisk. "I'll climb the ladder and if possible do a rub of the rest of the cartouche, and I'll check out the area and see if anything else presents itself," he says.

"I disagree," I say. "I think I should go up the ladder."

"No, Ellen. It's high and it'll be dangerous."

"Exactly! You're stronger and I'll need you on the ground to hold the ladder. You'll be able to control the ladder with me on it better than the other way around."

Although James looks like he wants to argue with me, he slowly nods his head in agreement.

"Alright. If we're not arrested by the time we get the ladder and get it up to the obelisk, you climb it and get the information."

"Now we have a plan!"

James shakes his head at me for my enthusiasm. "I don't know if you're brave or blind."

"And we have hours yet to kill before we can go back to the *Place*. I think we should go and see the Eiffel Tower," I offer to James.

"Ok. That would be great. It'll give us time to rehash the plan and see if we come up with any holes in it, and we certainly have the time," says James.

We finish our coffee and catch a cab for the Eiffel Tower. I'm excited about the plan for this evening and hope to find something new about the "Poppy Flowers" location. I'm also happy to get to show a part of Paris to James. I'm talking almost nonstop. I point out areas and buildings as we pass. James smiles indulgently at me and nods. He seems to enjoy my information and excitement.

When we get to the Eiffel Tower, we see there are hundreds of people in and around it. The area is beautiful and very large. We take the elevator of the Tower and I point out some attractions that we can see if we're in Paris long enough or if we have the opportunity to come back.

"Oh! If we are here long enough, we'll need to see the Pantheon! It's truly one of my favorites." I point out its location to James. "You can just make out a bit of it. There're beautiful statues and works of art and the building is lovely."

As we continue up the elevator, we look over Paris; the view from the top of the Tower is amazing. After a while, we decide to head down and find a café for lunch.

"Would you like to eat at the *Café du Trocadero*?" I ask him.

He smiles down at me and laughs, "Sure. Is that a good place?"

"Yes! It's very quintessentially Paris. Wonderful food, wonderful staff. We can sit at a table on the street and watch all the different people pass by."

When we get to the Café, we sit at a perfect table. The waiter, who is outfitted in a long white apron, takes our order and James asks me, "So the Pantheon is a favorite of yours?"

"Oh yes," I gush. "The architecture is amazing; majestic! And just the history — phenomenal! Construction began in 1757! Can you even wrap your head around that? I can't. It was a church and now it's a place of honor for the internment of great French citizens; the philosophers Voltaire and Jean-Jacques Rousseau and even Alexandre Dumas the author of <u>Three Musketeers</u>, is buried there. There are lots of people buried there, and beautiful marble statues are around every corner. Oh yes, James! It is a favorite. We'll go tomorrow, ok?"

James seems to enjoy my excitement as he replies, "I would love to have you show it to me."

The waiter brings our lunch and as we eat we watch the people and discuss the beauty of Paris. *This has turned out to be a perfect day*, I think, forgetting that danger is always close.

14

A little later, I stop talking and look around with a scowl. Something's wrong, as if a cloud passed over. I have a chill. I spin in my chair and glance down the street as a car passes and pulls away. The car has two men in it but I don't know them.

"What is it, El? Are you ok?"

"I don't know...yes, of course, I'm sure everything is fine," I stammer. "Just something weird." I lean back to watch the car turn a corner and disappear. My head is full of dark thoughts but I shake them off. I look at James and smile. "I'm good! In fact, I'm wonderful."

After we finish our lunch, we return to the hotel. We enter the elevator and James pulls me into his embrace. He steps me backwards to the wall, leans in and captures my mouth with his. He places one hand on my backside and runs the other up my ribcage to the edge of my breast. Placing my hands on his chest, I wrap my arms around his neck and grab a fistful of hair. I pull his head down, lean back and push my lower body into his. When James moves a leg between mine, I wrap my knee around it to pull him in. My only thought is, *Oh my! Oh my!* The physical pull from James continuously amazes me.

When the elevator dings on a floor, James lifts his head and kisses my nose. He steps half a step back, but keeps me in his arms. The door opens and an older gentleman in a suit enters the elevator. He gives us a curious look, but then smiles and says, "Paris is for lovers, no?"

I blush all the way from my hairline to my toes. James chuckles and says, "Yes, yes it is."

We arrive on our floor and rush laughing through the hotel door to trip into our room. I'm not good at it but I try to play the seductress. I gaze at James and walk slowly across the room to him. I begin to unbutton his shirt. He reaches to grasp the hemline of my shirt and pulls it over my head to throw it across the room. Laughing, I wrap my arms around him. I catch my breath as he clasps my wrists, spins me around and begins to kiss down my neck. He pulls my bra strap aside and continues down my shoulder. As he lets his hands roam free, he walks me toward the bed. With a small moan, my head falls back to his chest and I think, *Yes, Paris is for lovers.*

✶✶✶✶✶

As night falls, we prepare for our return to the obelisk. I double check my bag for my flashlight, a pencil and the papyrus paper. I make sure I'm wearing dark clothing to limit anyone's ability to see me at night and if necessary, to make evasion easier. James has also opted to dress darkly. Outside, a storm is beginning to roll in from the west; already the wind has picked up. We grab a taxi which drops us off a couple blocks from the *Place*. Heading that way, we're silent, each going over the plans in our heads.

Our plan, in addition to not getting caught, is to cut through the trees and undergrowth instead of the public route to the garage. Although it's a more direct route, it takes as long, or longer, because we aren't sure of our footing. As we near the garage, we slow and then stop. James places a finger to his lips and indicates with hand signals he wants me to wait by the trees. He moves toward the garage. With a gesture, he gives the "All's Okay" signal.

He bends toward the door and I approach him. In very short work, before I've even reached him, James opens the garage door. We listen intently but hear nothing except the rising storm so we step into the garage. We survey the interior and wait for an alarm to sound. When nothing happens, James shuts the door.

Both stalls in the garage are empty and when we lift the ladder it comes off the wall easily. As I pick up my end I'm thankful we don't have to transport it far. It's heavy! We open the door and maneuver ourselves out with the ladder. We've already decided that if time and the situation allow, we'll replace it and lock the garage. The perfect scenario will be for no one to know we'd been here. Stopping, we stare at the obelisk. *Dang!* I think. Unfortunately for us, the *Place de la Concorde* is lit at night. We hadn't thought of that. In particular, the tower and the two fountains on either side. Since there are buildings on the north side, buildings that include the French Foreign Ministry and the *Hotel de Crillon*, we'll stay to the south of the obelisk. The plan is to stay on the park side, get up and down as quickly as possible, NOT BE SEEN, and get away.

We near the monolith and I feel exposed. I continuously glance around, waiting for the French police to swarm us and put us under arrest. My hair, even in a ponytail, whips around my face as the storm builds. *Not the best weather to climb a tall ladder,* but I'm not going to back down now. We need to see what's on the cartouche with the images Angelo left for Maria.

When we near the fence surrounding the obelisk area, James and I lift the ladder over the barrier and then slip over it. I bend and lift my end and we hurry to the tower. "Okay," James leans into me and speaks directly into my ear. "Let's lift it and get it extended. I'll hold the bottom and you get up there and get what we need."

I nod and help him right the ladder. Luckily, the ground and the obelisk are level, so the ladder has a good foundation, but even with that going for us, the wind moves it before James gets a good handle on it.

"Ellen, the storm is really picking up. Are you sure this is a good idea?"

"I'm going up. We're not turning back now."

He leans into the wind and stands on the feet of the ladder. "You know what we need. Get up there."

I put my foot on the first rung of the ladder and look up; and up. *Ok, El,* I tell myself. *Let's do this girl! Up you go!*

MARCO

Marco watches the couple from the cover of the trees. When he was notified they'd left the hotel he was curious and then surprised, and to find they had not only returned to the park but stolen a ladder and were scaling the obelisk — he was almost impressed. Patiently, he watches them. He'll wait and see what, if anything, they come up with, but his focus is changed. The Lady wants all their information. She's grown tired of the wait and plans on finding the location of Angelo on her own, or at least with the help of the men she employs. The Americans don't know it yet, but they're out of the hunt. However, he isn't so stupid as to not let them finish this little adventure on the obelisk before he steps in.

ELLEN

I carefully climb the rungs of the ladder and realize I'm counting them. "Fifteen. Sixteen..." How far in the air I am I don't know, but I'm getting pretty high. The wind isn't cooperating — it gusts harder and harder the further I get. Just the act of tracing the complete cartouche is going to be a feat in gymnastics, but I don't want to chance it to memory. What if there's some little thing I don't remember that might make all the difference? As I near the top of the ladder, my hair creates a storm around my head. I reach with one hand and grab it, pushing it down the neckline of my jacket. It isn't a perfect solution, but it helps immeasurably. I find the cartouche with the matching pictures. It's an elongated oval and I clearly see the figure — what looks to be a profile of a man sitting, the triangle with its base and the tower. On the right side of the cartouche I see the finished product. It's the triangle again, a circle and a beetle. *Scarab, right? That's called a scarab.* I move up the ladder so I'm level with the image. I'll need both my hands to control the paper and pencil so I wrap my leg around the ladder and grip tightly. I dig into my bag for the thick pencil and the papyrus paper. The wind, like a malevolent spirit, tries to stop me as it grabs the paper and almost rips it from my grip. *That would be just great,* I think. I hold the paper with one hand against the wind and use the flat edge of the pencil to color the three figures into their spots on the cartouche. I can't see anything obvious on the obelisk but I don't trust my eyes. When I finish the trace of the entire area, I fold the paper and jam it into my bag with the pencil.

Hearing something, I glance down at James. *Whoa! Bad idea!* I'm further up the obelisk than I thought. James looks a long, way down. I think he's yelling something at me, but I can't hear him because of the wind. It's intent on ripping his words away. I scan the area and don't see anything amiss. James yells again and I decide to finish what I'm doing and get the hell down. I tighten my grip on the ladder with my legs and feel the area of the obelisk. I push as hard as I can and scrape my nails over the surface. I find nothing of interest and unable to think of anything else to do, I unwrap my leg and start down. The entire ladder shifts against the obelisk and with a small screech I grab it with both arms. I realize I'm praying a little. With my feet finally on the ground, I want to drop to my knees and kiss the pavement stones. I've no time, however, as James grabs my arm and yells into my ear, "We have company." I start and turn away from him, looking out over the park. At first, I don't see anything and I shake my head scanning the area. I begin to turn back to tell James he's crazy when I see a dark figure separate from the tree line. Now that my eyes are accustomed to the dark on dark of the shadows, I see two more. They advance on us from different parts of the park. "We need to get out of here," James yells.

"Which way should we go? They're all around us."

"Head for the Ministry. There's lights and traffic. Maybe we can lose them in the crowd."

I wrench aside as I hear the ladder hit the ground behind the tower. The sound seems to jumpstart my action as we turn north across the side of the park. I glance around again as we slide to the side of the obelisk. The figures are coming at a run. James grabs my arm and thrusts me ahead of him as he yells "RUN!" I take off and head for the brightly lit buildings on the other side of the avenue. I see cars and hear traffic but it seems a long way off. I hear James' feet pound behind me and I increase my speed. My heart beats a frantic rhythm from the exertion of running and the panic of being chased.

As we near the avenue, I chance a glimpse behind and see a group, all in dark clothing, as they close in on us. I'm determined to get away from them. Without hesitation, I plunge into the traffic on the avenue. Cars honk and swerve to avoid me. As I dodge the hood of a car, I feel a hand on my arm. I almost wrench it away only to realize it's James keeping me steady and pulling me down the street. Car horns blare as we run through the middle of the street and cross into the foot traffic on the other side. We race down the sidewalk, around and through people, for two more blocks when James grabs me and pulls me back into the flow of cars. He steps in front of a taxi causing it to screech to a halt to avoid hitting him. "Get in!" he gestures to me. I grab the door handle and yank it open just as the storm hits. Rain dumps as I climb into the vehicle. I've barely got myself seated when James jumps in with me. "GO!" he yells at the driver. "JUST DRIVE!" and we're off. I spin my body and peer out a rear window that runs with rainwater, scanning for any sign of the men, but they're gone.

Nervously, I wipe my wet face and push my hair from my forehead. "Who do you think they are? Can we risk returning to our hotel?" I'm trying to catch my breath and I'm speaking too fast and loud. I can tell James is thinking furiously.

"Let's swing in and grab our stuff. The cab can wait. We'll find another place to hole up while we decide what to do after that."

*****

An hour later, James and I enter another hotel and we're ready to drop. We returned to our original lodging and quickly grabbed our belongings only to find the taxi gone when we returned to the street. Luckily, we got another ride. We selected this place by chance and hope this randomness will allow us some anonymity from the people hunting us.

When we get to our new room, we drop our bags near the door and almost in a fugue state, wander the room.

"You know, we're going to have to find someone who can translate the hieroglyphics for us." After I state the obvious, I pull my laptop from my bag. I sit and fire it up. I use the parameters Paris and Egyptian and anything else I can think of. I need a shop to tell us what the hieroglyphics mean but I wonder if Angelo went somewhere special. How will we find the right place, if it even exists? It appears there are multiple stores near the obelisk dealing with Egyptian goods. We'll have to go to them, one by one.

James pushes a chair against the locked door and under the handle. He walks to me, and begins to strip his clothes as my eyes turn to him and I'm spell bound. "You ready for bed?"

I look at him from my seat and close the laptop. I move into his nearly naked body. I run my fingers through the hair at his nape and pull him down to me. I whisper, "I could use some sleep," and capture his lips with mine.

Even with my passion spent, I sleep fitfully. Who are those men? Is it as simple as breaking into the garage and stealing — borrowing, the ladder? Does it have something to do with Angelo and the "Poppy Flowers"? Other than the dead Joe Bell, nothing has been dangerous thus far. What the hell is going on and what should we do?

15

The next morning James jumps up and gives me a playful smack on the rump. Grabbing his jeans he tells me, "I've been thinking. I'm sure those men were from park security, that's why they didn't follow us any further. It just wasn't worth the effort." Nodding, almost to himself he adds. "I feel good about today and I'm sure we'll get information on the obelisk." As he pulls on his clothes he says, "I'm gonna run down the street for some croissants and hot cocoa at the plaza we passed." He sits on the bed. "Would you like anything else, Lovely Lady?"

I roll over and smile at him. "No, nothing else is required, Kind Sir." I laugh and roll onto my knees to wrap my arms around his neck from behind as he bends forward to tie his shoes. No matter what, I enjoy being with him.

"I'll be back in a jiff," he turns partway on the bed and gives me a kiss. He stands, grabs his wallet and heads out the door. "See you in a second…"

I jump out of bed and grab clean underwear, jeans and a t-shirt. Throwing on the clothes I pick up our belongings from the previous night. As I enjoy the rush of fresh air coming in the balcony, I hear a knock on the door. "Silly! Did you forget something?" I figure it must be James and pull it open. Suddenly, something hits the door hard from the outside and I'm knocked into a side table. I'm flung to the floor along with its contents. Confused, I attempt to scramble away from what I realize is two men. One advances on me and one searches the hall before closing the door. I'm getting to my feet when the memory hits me between the eyes:

I've just left Mr. Bell's house with the mirror in my bag. As I head for my car, I survey the street. I remember a car parked further down, a car with two men in it. And on the street in Paris, two men in a car as a chill shivers down my spine. Now, now I remember them clearly…and they're standing in my room. *Holy, Shit!* I think and try to scurry around the bed to the balcony, but the bigger man rushes me and grabs me by the hair, pulling me back. I give a little scream and reach for my hair with one hand, throwing an elbow at him with the other. He's a big hard man and my blow has little effect other than to make him angry. "Where is it?" he yells as he turns me to face him. Spittle flies onto me as he snarls and shakes me by my hair.

"What?" I grimace. "What do you want? I don't know what you want."

While I attempt to free my hair with one hand, I throw a punch at the man's throat. I catch him solidly and he coughs. Reacting, he bends over and drags me with him. As he stands up, he gives me a dangerous look. He lets go of my hair and backhands me to the ground.

"Marco," the other man says and steps forward. Marco stops for a split second and gives the other man a look of anger. I gape over my shoulder at them. One is big and brawny; he has a hard look and scars on his face. The other is smaller and looks just like a million other men — except he's standing in my hotel room. The noise in my brain is clambering. How to get out of this? What should I do? I feel the side of my face swelling and taste blood in my mouth from a split lip. I've never been hit before in my life and it's not an experience I want to repeat.

"Come little *Putana*," the big man says with a sneer. "We'll let you take it up with The Lady. She will like to meet you." I don't know who the LADY is and by the way he says it, I don't want to. He bends over and grabs me in a bruising grip on the upper arm. As he pulls me from the floor, I resist him out of instinct and I'm pushed into the bed face first. I shove myself up and as I try to maneuver away from the men, the big one grabs my hair again and flings me toward the door. My bare feet slip on the carpet and I go down, bruising my knees as I land.

Moaning, I pull myself up to the door and attempt to grab the knob. Marco moves behind me and flattens me with his body. The smell of his sweat and breath mix with the smell of my fear. I suck in a great gasp of air to scream when the man puts his hand over my mouth. The rush of adrenaline in my body makes me lightheaded and I push off the door to dislodge him, kicking with my feet towards his shins.

"Stop," he says threateningly and presses the bulk of his weight into me. I can't breathe or move and squirm helplessly in an attempt to do something. "You will behave or I will have to subdue you. Do you understand?"

I realize this form of resistance will gain me nothing. I nod my head against the door. I need to get out of this. I need to warn James. But I don't need to be SUBDUED by Marco. Marco grabs my arm and pulls me back into the room. I remain compliant as I swing my gaze frantically about for any avenue of escape. The smaller man grabs my bag from the floor and opens the door carefully. He looks up and down the hallway and pulls the door wide, gestures with a nod that the way is clear. Marco steps through the door and drags me with him, then heads toward the stairwell. The hotel door closes behind us and soon we're going down the stairs. The stairway is cold in my t-shirt and my bare feet are freezing on the steps as the man hustles me down the stairs, but that's the least of my worries.

JAMES

James feels good. It promises to be a good day and they're well on their way to figuring out another clue. He picks up some croissants when he remembers the little flower shop he'd glimpsed down the street. With a smile, he thinks of Ellen's face when he brings her flowers; all women love flowers, right? He turns and jogs across the street, walks the block or so to the flower shop. At the shop, he realizes he doesn't know her favorite flower. So many things to learn about this woman. She's funny, intelligent and passionate. What an amazing woman. He decides to get her a bouquet that's a combination of all flowers: a combination that reminds him of her — a mixture of many things.

When he returns to their room, James is running on a high. As he opens the door he calls out, "Ma Bella! I have sustenance for you...." He stops mid stride and looks around the room as his cop instincts kick in. The bag and flowers are dropped as he flattens his back to the wall. He reaches for his nonexistent side arm and quickly realizes he's weaponless. James scans the hall and seeing nothing closes the door quietly. "Ellen!" he calls out. He surveys the room from the entryway and notes the overturned table and the bed sheets pulled to the carpet on one side. The balcony door is open with a breeze blowing the gauzy draperies. Through the balcony door, he hears noises from the street; cars drive by, people yell to each other, but in the room, all is silent. James slides into the room, does a quick check of the bathroom and determines he's alone. Ellen's gone and it doesn't look like she went willingly.

James kicks himself for forgetting even for a moment why they're here. He calms himself and picks up the phone to call the local authorities. He explains the disappearance of Ellen and her possible abduction and is quickly transferred to a French detective. James introduces himself and fills Detective Bernard in on some of what's happened and his suspicions. The detective instructs James to stay there. James goes through the room while he waits for the French police to arrive, he touches nothing. Immediately, he notices that although Ellen's bag is gone, her cell phone is still plugged in on the dresser, which adds to his anxiety. When he finds a spot of blood on the sheets his breath stops and then comes so fast he's almost panting. *How much is she hurt? Who's done this? Where is she?*

He hears a knock on the door and hurries to pull it open to see a plain clothes detective with a uniformed officer behind him. He opens the door wide and asks, "Detective Bernard?"

"Yes, and you are Detective Russell?" the French man asks.

"I am. Please come in."

Detective Bernard enters the room, studying it. He asks James to recap the story. "And you think Ms. Thompsons' disappearance has something to do with the missing "Poppy Flowers"?" he asks James incredulously.

"Yes. I know it sounds a bit farfetched but we have a series of clues that led us this far." James goes to where he and Ellen chose to hide the items related to their search. After their flight from the men, they decided to be more careful in case the danger was real. Retrieving the packet of notes, cards and other clues, James hands the pieces to Detective Bernard and fills him in a little on the history of "Poppy Flowers". "According to the media, when the "Poppy Flowers" disappeared two Italians were stopped and questioned at the airport. They'd been at the Egyptian museum earlier in the day and acted oddly. Because of the first notes and later items, we think Angelo and Maria were the two Italians. Since then we've discovered other clues that led us here." Detective Bernard looks at the items and reads the notes. He shakes his head with disbelief.

"Incredible. This is truly incredible. I remember when the painting went missing in Egypt; it made all the papers. But how did this note end up in a mirror in America? Who is this Joe Bell who had the mirror?"

James shakes his head and sighs, "We don't really know about Joe Bell. All our evidence indicates he didn't exist prior to four years ago. We don't know where he came from or how he came by these items. We've tracked Angelo to this point and plan on continuing to see if we can find him or the painting."

Just then, James' phone rings in his pocket. He looks at the screen but doesn't recognize the number. He raises his eyebrows in question. Detective Bernard nods yes, and steps close to James to hear the conversation. James pushes the accept button and puts the phone to his ear. "Yes?" he asks.

"Ah, Detective Russell," a woman's silky voice says. "I believe you have something I want; and conversely, I have something you want. Funny how life works out sometime, no?"

"Where is Ellen?" he asks her.

"Oh your woman is quite well, feisty though. I'm afraid my man had to discipline her a bit. A shame, I'm sure, but she's no worse for wear." Her voice is smooth, cultured and evil. James' mind begins to think of all the things that could've happened and still be happening to Ellen.

"I want her back," he insists.

"Well good. At least we're in agreement. You want her back and I want my property returned to me."

Impatiently James snaps, "What is it you want?"

The woman laughs a little and says, "Oh, Detective Russell, please don't be obtuse. My notes from Angelo and the clues he left for me. Everything you've collected up to this point, in fact, and the location of the "Poppy Flowers". My men found my mirror in Ms. Thompson's apartment in America, so I know you and she have the note and my correspondence with my brother and you're on the trail of my Angelo. All you need to do is give them to me and I'll return her to you. Simple?"

"Where and when?" he asks. Nothing else matters but getting Ellen back. "And I want to speak to Ellen. I need to know she's alright." He catches Detective Bernard's eye and the detective nods his approval. He feels his anger heat but takes a deep breath and remains calm.

James hears a commotion on the other side of the phone and then Ellen's voice. "James? James, I'm ok."

"Ellen! Ellen, I'm so sorry...I'm coming to get you, Baby. It'll be okay." His body tenses with the need to act but there's nowhere to go and nothing to do.

"James," she gulps and in a whisper he can barely make out, says. "My place, my favorite place…"

The woman comes back on. "We'll contact you soon, Detective Russell. Be prepared," and hangs up.

"The Pantheon," James says as he looks from his phone to Detective Bernard. "She's in the Pantheon. I don't know where in the building, but I'm sure that's what Ellen meant." Detective Bernard nods his head and pulls out his phone to place a call. James hears him confer with someone who seems to be his superior. When he gets off the phone he turns to James, "I've spoken to my Lieutenant and he'll send backup for us. We can be there in a few moments and will assess the area to best determine where Ms. Thompson is being held."

They hurry out of the hotel room and down the elevator. The French police officers, with James, climb into a police sedan. Detective Bernard pulls the car into the street and accelerates toward the other side of town.

ELLEN

When the men take me, I'm shocked and no matter how I try I can't find any way to free myself. Soon the three of us are in a van (all I can think is not to allow an abductor to take you to a secondary location and how stupid I am to be in this van) and we head to the other side of Paris. When the van stops, Salvi slides open the side door, jumps out and turns to me. I know I must be pale and I'm shaking with shock and cold. My hair is snarled from Marco's hands and my feet are filthy from the floors. Salvi holds out his hand. "*Perdere* Thompson, please come with me." When I remain pushed against the far wall of the van he adds, "Unless you would rather Marco make you come out of the van?" My eyes are large and my breath comes in little pants. I attempt to quickly assess which is the greater threat. I see Marco as he comes around the front of the van after exiting the driver's seat, so I push through Salvi's hand without taking it and climb from the van.

I step into the late afternoon sunlight and lift my face to its warmth to stare at the building where we've arrived. "The Pantheon," I mutter quietly. What're the odds?

"*Perdere*?" Salvi indicates he wishes me to follow him around the back of the building. Marco is directly behind me. Quickly, I scan this location again. I feel an almost overpowering need to run, to just try it. The desperation is eating at my gut. As if he senses my indecision, Marco steps up so his body is just touching mine. I jump a little and as I comply and move forward I peek over my shoulder at Marco. He looks down at me with blank eyes, dead of all emotion and I feel completely trapped.

We round the building and a wind catches us and blows my hair over my face, chilling me even further. At the back of the building, Salvi walks to a small door and knocks. I shiver and my mind races; *Jesus, Jesus*, I think. *What am I to do*? The door opens to another man who looks at the three of us before he moves out of the way.

We walk through the door and into a long domed room. I hear the footfalls of the men's boots echo all around as we approach the other end. I realize we've entered the crypt from the back side and proceed toward the front. I'm overwhelmed. It's like my life is running in reverse. I've been in this building and the crypt many times, but never have I entered through the back. *Why are we here of all places? Who's the Lady they spoke of? What's going to happen to me? Is James ok? How can I get myself out of this and keep him safe? How can he find me?*

The man in front of me, Salvi, stops at a large metal door and pulls it open. It groans and screeches unpleasantly as light from the inside pours into the darkness. I squint as I'm momentarily blinded by the light from the other room. When I don't immediately follow Salvi through the doorway Marco bumps me from behind which causes me to trip into the room. Righting myself, I look up to see an amazingly beautiful woman within. *The Lady*, I think.

Marco grabs my arm, again, and pulls me forward to shove me into a chair. The action almost overturns the chair and threatens to spill me onto the floor. I catch myself and sit straight; give him a dirty look and can't resist saying, "You're fast becoming tiresome, big boy." Marco just looks back at me with a blank look but the woman gives a deep chuckle and walks to me to run her hand over my cheek and hair causing me to cringe and pull back from her.

"Ms. Thompson, welcome. I am Maria Cabana and I do believe you have something of value of mine."

Maria Cabana? I think. I look at the woman and say, "I'm sorry. I don't know who you are. Maybe there's been some mistake. I won't tell anyone if I can just leave..." My words are ripped from me when Marco steps forward and backhands me again. I catch the chair before it topples. My whole upper body leans over the arm of the chair. As I sit up, I glare at Marco, but don't say anything. I see Salvi by the door and wonder if it's possible for me to get around four people, out a doorway and away from here.

"Let us try this again, shall we? Where is my note? My cards and correspondence from Angelo? And if you please, the location of the "Poppy Flowers." As she speaks, Maria walks around me in a circle. I track her with turns of my head and body as I attempt to keep her in sight, as if she were a poisonous snake or a mad dog. When I don't answer right away, Marco grabs my hair, wrenching my head back. I feel my neck pop and try to talk. He releases the pressure a little and twists my head to the side. Maria has a small smile and an expression an indulgent parent might use while they watch a small boy torture a fly by ripping off its wings. "Well? Note, cards, painting..." she says again.

Later...
I lift myself to my feet again. I wobble and hurt but am less and less willing to give this woman anything. The worse they are to me, the less willing I am to talk. A trait my father liked to refer to as 'Stubborn as a Mule'. I get a nice mouthful of saliva and blood

together and spit it in Maria's general direction. This small bit of rebellion is all I can muster at this point, but I have to do something. *Italian Bitch!* I think to myself.

Maria takes a deep breath and gestures to Marco. "Call him," she says. Marco dials a number and hands the phone to Maria. She waits a moment. "Ah, Detective Russell. I believe you have something I want; and conversely, I have something you want. Funny how life works out sometime, no?" I immediately perk up.

Maria chuckles and smiles into the phone. I listen to her discuss the situation as if I'm not even present. I hear James' voice faintly but can't make out what he says.

"Well good. At least we're in agreement. You want her back and I want my property returned to me." After she listens for a moment, Maria's mouth purses with displeasure. She continues to discuss the "Poppy Flowers" with James and it's apparent she thinks he'll give her the cards and items in exchange for me. After she listens for a moment, Maria looks toward me. She thrusts the phone at me and demands, "Talk to him. Tell him you are alive."

"James," I say shakily. "James, I'm ok."

"Ellen, Ellen I'm so sorry...I'm coming to get you, Baby. It'll be okay." Just hearing his voice breaks me in ways Maria and Marco never can. I begin to cry and tighten my resolve.

I whisper, "James, my place, my favorite place..." I barely get the words out of my mouth when the phone is ripped away from me. I don't know if James heard me or not. With a sob, I drop my head.

"We'll contact you soon, Detective Russell. Be prepared," Maria says into the phone. She hangs up and hands it to Marco.

"Well," she says snidely as she circles me. "It seems your man is more than willing to give up my items for your safe return. How touching. It makes your resistance look even more foolish." As she throws me a last condescending look, Maria walks away toward the door. Over her shoulder she says to Marco, "Tie her up and watch her, we'll be moving soon."

No, I think.

✶✶✶✶✶

MARIA

Maria's excited by the prospect of finally getting to the "Poppy Flowers". *Soon,* she thinks. *It will all be mine.* How little she resembles that woman five years ago who was so in love with Angelo and a favorite of her padre's. Everything had fallen together and then fallen apart. Egypt had been so wonderful; until the "Poppy Flowers"...

MARIA 2010...

Ah! I love to visit new places and Egypt is one of my favorites! Maria thinks as she prepares for their day. She knows Angelo isn't happy to visit the museum, he wants to spend the morning in the busy, noisy marketplace. Oh well? Maybe if they have time before they need to get to the airport, they can go to the marketplace. Maria heard about the Mohamed Mahmoud Khalil Museum and is eager to see the famed artwork on display. She smiles at Angelo and slips her arm through his to head for the bus.

At the museum, there's a photographer who walks the grounds and offers to take peoples pictures. It's fun and fancy and they print them right on the spot. Maria loves the picture of her and Angelo. She's going to put it in her rooms to commemorate their visit to Egypt. In the museum, Maria leads the way through the different rooms. She's in awe of the beautiful paintings by all of the masters. How can one man amass so many beautiful and costly items? She walks through a particularly long and grand room and realizes Angelo isn't with her.

"Angelo?" she says, and looks around. Abruptly, he comes into the room, grabs her by the arm and says they need to leave. "What's wrong, Angelo? Are you unwell?" Maria asks with concern. Her brow furrows as she looks at him. When she realizes she scowled, she immediately relaxes her face.

"Yes, Maria," he answers. "I'm feeling ill. We need to leave right away," and he moves her along the corridor.

On the way out, Maria suggests they stop by the restrooms so he can wet his face. He's sweating profusely and she's concerned he might faint. She feels true concern as she paces the hallway until he reappears. Soon they leave the museum, but instead of heading toward the bus, Angelo veers off and heads to the back of the building. Maria follows at a quick pace and calls out, "Angelo! Slow down!" but he continues out of her sight.

As she comes around the corner, Maria sees Angelo get up from the grass. He dusts off his pants and has his jacket rumpled in his hand. He holds the jacket against his body and grabs her arm again, heading toward the bus.

"Angelo, what's the matter? What are you doing?" she pants as she tries to keep up.

"Nothing, Maria," he answers. "Let's get back to the hotel and get our belongings."

The entire way back to the hotel, Angelo sweats and watches out the window anxiously. He jumps whenever a car accelerates by the bus and once a police vehicle passes them and he almost stands up; he leans into the window to watch it pass. Maria watches him, wondering. At the hotel they pack hurriedly and catch a taxi.

Angelo seems to calm at the airport and she thinks he might be feeling better. His breathing becomes more normal and instead of grabbing her and hustling her along, he takes her hand as usual. When they near the security checkpoint she feels him tense up; the arm he has around her becomes tight and uncomfortable. All of a sudden, without warning, a large woman pushes in front of them and causes Angelo to trip into her. The woman gives him a rude look and goes through the check point.

With a flurry of commotion security officers surrounded them. Maria looks at the officers and in a shaking voice asks Angelo, "What's happening?"

"Just cooperate, Maria. Everything will be alright," he reassures her, but she doesn't believe him. Angelo is back to being pale and sweaty. She thinks they're in real trouble.

They're led by an officer into a back room and questioned about the disappearance of a painting that occurred at the time they were at the museum. Maria watches Angelo, but doesn't speak or ask any questions. What has he done? Does this have something to do with his strange behavior this morning?

The guards search their luggage and threaten them but in the end they let them go. Quickly, they hurry down the boarding bridge to their plane to Italy and home. Maria takes a deep breath and looks for their seat. As she walks down the aisle, she passes the rude lady from the security check and thinks, *if they want to question someone, they should ask her how she can be so rude.*

*****

Maria comes back to the present and thinks how the memory of that day used to make her sad and nostalgic for Angelo. Now it's one more thing that makes her angry. It seems these days everything makes her angry. Ever since her Padre realized not only had Angelo left, but with him he'd taken the painting "Poppy Flowers". Her father had been obsessed with the artwork of Adolphe Monticelli and his link to Van Gogh for as long as she could remember. Somehow, somewhere he imagined they were descended from the Monticelli line and the legacy was rightly his. He was insane, if you asked her. He'd even had possession of the "Poppy Flowers" back in 1978, but then got sloppy in Kuwait and the authorities recovered it. When he found out Angelo stole the painting, and it had been so close, he was excited, manic. Then he found out Angelo left and took the painting with him and he had been...not happy. He'd struck Maria; something she would never have imagined from her indulgent Papa. When his ring sliced her skin and she experienced the pain and betrayal, she'd changed, both physically and emotionally. She still remembers the feel of her flayed skin and warm blood on her fingers. That day her beloved Padre sealed his fate.

Two Years Ago...

Maria looks in the mirror and a tear runs down the scar on the side of her face. She knew when her Padre hit her years ago she would never forgive him or forget his action. Every day she's reminded of his brutality. Every day she's reminded she's no longer the most beautiful woman people, any person, has ever seen. Well, her vengeance is about to be fulfilled. She's sent away his only son and he'll never come back. And now her Padre is bedridden, frail.

After she pulls on a dressing gown, Maria quietly opens the door to her bedroom. She creeps down the hallway and silently enters her father's room. As usual, his room has a musty, medicine-like odor to it. She wrinkles her nose in distaste. There's a lamp burning next to his bed and she sees the rise and fall of his chest as he sleeps fitfully. *Good*, she thinks. *I hope his rest is spoiled by the thought of the wreck his life has become*. She creeps to his bed and stands to watch her father. Something about her presence must penetrate his sleep for he gives a start and opens his eyes. "Maria, my jewel..." he says groggily. Maria picks up a pillow. She looks down at her once beloved father and places it over his face. She has to lay over him as he begins to thrash about, but he's no longer a strong and viral man. Within moments, he quiets. Maria stays where she is for a minute more. She wishes she could end his life in a violent way, but there must be no uproar to his death. She stands, removes the pillow, fluffs it and places it back on the bed. She stares down at her dead father for so long she begins to feel the chill of the room. She turns on her heel and heads back to the door. When she gets to her room, she climbs into bed and falls immediately into a deep restful sleep.

*****

Maria blinks and pulls herself out of her memories, memories of a different time. She watches the American tied to a chair across the room and knows she's no longer a woman under a man's thumb. She's done what's necessary to be whom she needs and wants to be. With her father's death and Joseph's disappearance, she became the head of the Cabanas family. SHE is in charge of everything and being in charge is just where she's meant to be. She did find, however, she now has her own obsession with the "Poppy Flowers". Not for the same reasons as her father and certainly not the insanity of Angelo. No, she wants the painting just to have it. To own something none of the men in her life can hang onto. Soon she will call James Russell and set up a place to meet. He'll think he's made a good trade, her items for the woman, but she has no intention in allowing the Americans to leave with their lives. If there's one thing she's learned it's being a loose end ends badly. Angelo should have thought of that before he put that painting before her.

ANGELO 2010...

Angelo looks at Maria and smiles. She's so pretty and he loves her so much. It really doesn't matter that he doesn't want to go to the museum today. If Maria wants to go, he'll go — and he'll be glad to be with her.

"*Si, si bella signora!*" he laughingly says and pulls her close. "We'll go see your little museum today."

Maria smiles knowingly and grabs her bag. "Let's go then lazy bones or we'll miss the bus."

Angelo and Maria have been in Cairo for a couple of days and leave later that day on a flight back to Italy. He wanted to spend the morning in the busy marketplace, but Maria likes the quiet and the art of a museum.

As they speed through the city of Cairo, Angelo sees the marketplace from afar. *Oh well*, he thinks and looks at his Maria, *I would give her the moon if I could*.

The Mohamed Mahmoud Khalil Museum is a beautiful building: it's three stories, with large stately windows and manicured grounds. Maria reads to him from the pamphlet the bus driver gave them.

"At Signor Khalil's death his wife endowed his collection to the government of Egypt. Even though it's a private collection, it still rivals most European National Collections."

Before going into the museum, Maria pulls Angelo to a photographer and has their picture taken. Angelo never likes to have his photo taken, but Maria insists and he'll do anything for her. As Angelo and Maria wander through the museum it's very quiet. They arrived on the bus with a small tour, but soon everyone goes their own way. They only see one other person and twice see some security. Maria's in awe of the artwork. Great impressionists hang on the walls: Gauguin, Monet, Renoir and many others. Angelo trails behind her, his thoughts on the trip home.

As they continue through the rooms, a particular painting catches his eye. Angelo doesn't understand the draw but is unable to pull away. It hangs above a settee and is small, about a foot by a foot in an ornate frame. He hears Maria as she moves away and knows she'll look for him soon but he can't move, can't make his feet follow her. Almost in a trance he moves toward the painting. There's no one around and the thought *now's my chance*! flickers through his head. Angelo glances about and steps up onto the settee. He reaches into his pants pocket and pulls out a small knife he keeps to open packages. Quickly, he cuts the painting out of the frame, rolls it up, wraps it in his jacket and drops it out an open window. It lands three stories down behind some shrubs. He studies the outside area quickly, then scurries off to find Maria, his mind no longer on the return home, but on the painting.

Maria's in the next room where she admires a large Monet.

"Ah Angelo, there you are. Isn't this beautiful?" she asks dreamily.

"Come, Maria. We have to leave." Angelo tells her hurriedly. He begins to pull her by the arm toward the exit and looks furtively about. "We must go now."

"Angelo! What are you doing? We have plenty of time to get to the airport before our plane." She shakes him off and looks at him intently. "Why are you sweating? Are you feeling alright?"

"No, no," he says. "I'm unwell. We have to leave immediately!"

"All right, Angelo. I'm sorry you're not well. Let's stop by the restrooms before we catch the bus."

Angelo feels as if he's going to faint and thinks splashing some water on his face will be a good idea. He lets Maria lead him to the restrooms. Moments later they're outside the museum and heading around the side.

"Where are you going now, Angelo? The bus stop is out front."

"I have one thing to do," he replies. Maria can barely keep up with him as he walks quickly around the side of the museum.

"Angelo! Slow down!"

As Angelo comes around to the side of the building, he drops to his knees and pulls his jacket and the painting from under the shrub. He stands and cradles it next to his body as Maria catches up to him. He takes her arm and starts for the bus stop.

When they get on the bus without being detained or questioned Angelo can't believe his luck. *It's MINE!* he thinks. *It's mine and I'll never give it back.* The entire way to the hotel he watches the traffic. He waits for the *Carabineers* to stop the bus and arrest him. *What have I done?* he wonders, but even now the painting calls to him to take it out; to look at it...

When they get to the hotel Maria and Angelo hurriedly pack their bags. Maria looks at him with concern and alarm.

"Angelo. Please Angelo. Speak with me. Tell me what's wrong."

Angelo shakes his head but will not, cannot explain. "Just hurry, Maria. We must get to the airport."

Angelo locks himself in the bathroom and rolls the painting up as tightly as he dares. He wraps newspaper around the outside and ties it with spare shoe laces. When he's finished, he places the package carefully in his carry-on luggage.

Maria knocks on the bathroom door. "Angelo! The taxi's here. We need to go."

He opens the door and picks up his luggage. "Let's go."

We just might make it, Angelo thinks as the line moves toward the security checkpoint to the boarding area for their plane. The security personnel on guard are preoccupied with other things and don't look like they're taking the time to really check anyone or their luggage. He can feel the sweat drip down his face and run down the small of his back, and tells himself to hold it together. Soon they'll be in Italy and he'll have what has become so important.

"Next!" The security guard looks right at him and all of a sudden Angelo can see himself in an Egyptian prison.

"*Pardon Moi!*" a well-dressed, heavy set woman says as she pushes her way into the line between Angelo and the guard.

What a maleducata donna, Angelo thinks with a sneer on his face. But wait...this woman, this rude woman's bag bulges open and she'll bully her way through the security. Without any hesitation, Angelo pulls the painting out of his bag and fakes a stumble. He shoves it into her bag. *There*! he smiles to himself. *We'll all get to Italy and I'll get my painting back*. Angelo feels very smart as he puts his arm around Maria and walks to security.

Out of nowhere security agents surround them.

"What's happening?" Maria looks at Angelo with alarm.

"It'll be alright, Maria," he soothes her. "Just cooperate."

The security guards take them to a back room and push them into seats.

"Were you at the Mohamed Mahmoud Khalil Museum today?" asks a very large, angry man in a commander's uniform.

"Yes, yes we were," says Maria, and looks at Angelo in confusion. "What's this all about?"

"While you were at the museum, a painting by Van Gogh disappeared," he all but shouts at them. "What do you know about this painting? You left very abruptly during your visit. You didn't stay with your group."

"We don't know anything," Angelo answers. "We went to the museum before we left Cairo, but I became ill. We left early so I could rest before we came to the airport, that's all."

The Commander turns to one of the officers. "Search their luggage. We'll find the painting!"

Angelo and Maria watch as the officers open their luggage and tear everything out of it. They don't protest for fear of being kept in Egypt. When everything is searched, the commander turns and looks at them.

"We have no reason to detain you. Get on your plane and consider yourselves lucky."

When Angelo and Maria leave the interrogation room they're shaken. Angelo puts his arm around Maria and leads her toward the boarding area.

"What was that about, Angelo?"

"Nothing, Maria. Let's get on the plane."

As they board and move to their seats, Angelo notices the rude French woman a few seats ahead of theirs. Her bags aren't on the floor in front of her so they must be in the overhead compartment. He scans the open compartments as they move to their seats and notes her distinctive polka dot bag. He places his carry-on bag in the same compartment. During the flight he'll get his painting.

"It worked!" he breathes a sigh of relief.

16

JAMES

Detective Bernard, James and an entire French SWAT team pull up two blocks from the Pantheon. When James steps out of Detective Bernard's sedan he's impressed by the tactical precision of the SWAT team as they deploy. Even without the information on the lost Van Gogh painting, or the murdered man in America, they still have a kidnapped American woman on French soil that needs to be dealt with seriously. For this, James is very appreciative.

Detective Bernard invites James to accompany him into the back of a surveillance van of the National Police force. They're assessing the situation and building with Doppler radar sensors. One officer turns away from his instrument as they step in. He looks at his superior, "*Capitaine*, there appear to be five people in the Pantheon."

"Very good, Officer Martin. Can you tell if one appears to be a hostage?" the Captain asks.

As he looks back at the screen, the young officer replies, "Yes, Sir, possibly. One is seated apart from the others. That one isn't moving freely."

The Captain notices James and Detective Bernard at that moment. "Adrien. Good to see you," he says to Detective Bernard and shakes his hand. "It does appear we have a serious situation here. Even if there isn't a hostage…" He pauses as James starts to speak and puts up a hand to halt him, "and I'm not saying there isn't, but even if there wasn't, we take seriously the breaking and entering of a national monument. We have the building surrounded and we'll enter shortly."

Detective Bernard nods. "This is Detective Russell from America," he says with an indication at James. "The woman kidnapper says she'll contact him again. This may come in handy to triangulate her location among the other bodies."

"Yes," the Captain says with a nod as he shakes James's hand. "We're set to go in 30 minutes. If she doesn't contact you in that time, we'll move without it. Give your phone to Officer Martin and he'll link it to our computers. We'll be able to hear the conversation if and when she calls you." He nods at James and turns back to the techs.

"Excuse me, Captain," James says which causes the police officer to turn back around. "What assurances have you made for Ellen's safety? I'd like to suit up and go in with your team."

The Captain gives James a nod and says, "I understand your concern for Ms. Thompson, detective. However, I'm unable to have you enter the premises with the SWAT team. I cannot have another civilian — even an American Police Officer — put into harm's way." Although James understands this and the politics of it, he can't just stand here while Ellen is in danger. He has to do something…with the thought that he'll come up with a plan, James gives the French officer his phone.

ELLEN

Maria stops pacing and walks over, stopping in front of me. They've zip tied me to the chair by my feet and with my hands behind my back. My head hangs forward and my hair is covering my face. I haven't been given anything to drink in hours, which is probably good since no one has offered me the use of a bathroom either. I see Maria's feet but don't have the energy or inclination to lift my head and look at the woman, and with my feet tied to the chair I'm unable to kick at her.

Maria speaks to Marco. "Call him," she says. "Let's see what he has to say."

JAMES

In the police van, James' cell phone, which has been returned to him, begins to ring. He lifts it and looks at the screen. He shows it to Detective Bernard. Speaking to the Captain, Detective Bernard says, "It's her. It's the kidnapper."

The phone rings once more and the French Captain moves next to James. "Ok. Answer it and try to keep her on the phone. We'll get a fix on her location."

James presses accept and says, "Yes?"

"Ah, Detective Russell," Maria says sweetly. "I thought you weren't going to answer. Perhaps you've found another woman who isn't so much trouble?"

"I want to speak to Ellen," James states. "I want to speak to her right now."

"You know, Detective," Maria pauses and then goes on, "I've never been very good with men who make demands of me."

"I have what you asked for, but first I want to speak to Ellen." He hesitates and then says, "Please."

James can practically hear Maria smile as she says, "How nicely you ask when you want to." The phone is covered but he strains and can hear Maria say, "Cut her hands loose and give her the phone."

"James?"

He can hear the fatigue in Ellen's voice. *How much longer can this continue?*

"Ellen! Ellen are you all right?" he asks.

"You know," she says to him with a sigh, "I've had better days."

"It's going to be fine, El. It'll all be over very soon. I'm so proud of you. It'll all be over soon."

"Oh. How sweet," Maria says into his ear causing James to scowl at his phone. He looks at the technicians and the Captain and receives a thumb up. "Where do you want to do this, lady?" James asks with a sneer in his voice.

"You will go to the *La Menagerie*." Maria tells him.

James' brow furrows. *What is she talking about*? He looks at Detective Bernard who shrugs and shakes his head in confusion. "Ok?" James says with hesitation. "I'll find it. What do I do when I get there?"

"We'll meet you at the Bird House. You'll bring my property and I'll give you Ms. Thompson."

James lets Maria talk about the meet and how they'll exchange Ellen for Angelo's clues. He knows that it doesn't matter what she thinks will happen, the police are outside the building ready to arrest her and her men.

The police van is a flutter of activity in their preparation to take the kidnappers as they exit the building. The officers watch the heat signatures and can see them come together in the room. They move through the crypt toward the rear door. The French police have the building surrounded so James knows Maria and her men won't get away, but that doesn't guarantee Ellen's safety. The police move out and fall into place. He follows a group that heads to the back of the building. This is where the kidnappers appear to be moving to. He stands at the rear of the building with his back against the wall. A couple of the SWAT officers look at him quizzically but no one says anything. James wonders, *do they think because he'd been in the command center that he had permission to be on site?* He really doesn't care. He just knows he needs to get his hands on Ellen. He needs to ensure she's safe, to touch her again.

The door opens from the inside and all of the officers tense. Two men step out and then he sees a small dark haired woman, *Maria*, he thinks. Close behind her is a large man with Ellen in his grip. His heart contracts to see her. He's never seen her look so downtrodden. Her head is forward and her hair hangs obscuring her face. The man gives her arm a jerk and as she hisses, Ellen pulls back, throws a punch at him and hits him in the nose. At that, everything happens at once. The man gives a loud bellow, grabs his nose and pulls Ellen into his body. The two men and Maria turn and the SWAT jump forward.

"*Arret!*" the Captain yells. For a split second everyone freezes, and then everything moves into hyper-drive.

The two men in the front attempt to elude the police and run into the grounds that surround the Pantheon. Maria stands still as if the activity is beneath her. In an attempt to use Ellen as a shield, the large man pulls her with him and moves back toward the building, but the police have closed that exit.

ELLEN

I jerk my eyes up at a loud roar and see James leap at Marco. He hits him hard, causing him to release my arm, but the three of us crash to the ground. I roll twice and come up on my hands and knees next to where the men are brawling. In the darkness, I can just make out James as he sits on Marco's chest and hits him in the face repeatedly, over and over until the police pull him off.

I stare over the top of Marco, who's turned over and handcuffed by the police, and see James. *How did he come to be here? What's happening?* He pulls himself up and limps over to help me stand. As he takes me into his arms, he buries his face in my neck and holds on tight.

I give a shudder and wrap my arms around his waist and mutter, "James, James." He attempts to keep me turned away from the commotion as he looks at the kidnappers but I need to see. Three men, including Marco, are laid out on the ground with their hands and feet zip tied. The Captain is with an officer and a handcuffed Maria asking her questions we can't hear. She's ignoring the Captain as she stares straight at us with a killing look on her face.

A detective walks to James and me. He's pleasant looking: about my height, middle aged with gray hair. He's in a suit and a light trench coat with an unbuckled belt that flaps as he walks. "Detective Russell, Ms. Thompson, if I can have you come with me, we have some questions for you. We'll get the formalities finished as soon as possible. I'm sure you wish to relax and recoup."

"Of course," James says. His gaze doesn't leave Maria as she stares at us. "Thank you, detective for your assistance in getting Ellen back safely."

"Yes, yes. We're always glad for a happy outcome in a situation such as this."

The three of us turn from the police and kidnappers and make our way to a van that James explains is a Command Station. He helps me sit in one of the chairs and leans on the counter beside me with his hand on my shoulder. The detective makes tea in the small microwave at the front. He brings it and a blanket to me and hands the blanket to James. As James squats in front of me, he opens the blanket and urges me to lean forward. He wraps it around my shoulders. I watch him as he takes care of me. My mind is in a fog and it feels as if I'm watching the three of us from a distant place.

James takes the tea from the detective and blows on it gently. He places it in my hands, placing his hands over mine. "This'll warm you up, Baby," he says to me.

As he helps me to lift the cup, James says, "Take a sip, Sweetie. It'll help calm you and we'll talk with Adrien. He helped me find you." He smiles at me and adds, "He's a real nice cop."

As I take a small sip of the tea, I smell jasmine and mint. I lean forward and place my forehead against James'. "This is real, right?" I ask quietly nodding my head. "You're really here?"

James tips my head up and kisses me gently on the lips. He looks me straight in the eyes and says, "Yes. Yes, Ellen. I'm here now and you're safe."

Finally I realize it's over and start to cry softly. James takes the tea away and hands it to Detective Bernard. He leans in and holds onto me. Behind him, I hear the detective set the tea down and step out of the van.

✶✶✶✶✶

Detective Adrien Bernard sits across from James and me in the command van and finishes his immediate questions. "Thank you for your patience, Ms. Thompson. I know you're hurt and tired. We have *en Technicien medical* here to look at you. Then you may leave, but I will need you to come to the *poste de police* tomorrow. We have further questions."

"Of course, Detective Bernard," I reply. "Thank you for your help and understanding."

Detective Bernard smiles, "You're a fine lady, Ms. Thompson." He gets up and nods at James. Detective Bernard opens the van door and invites the medical technician to enter, then he steps out. James picks up my hand, he holds it between his as the technician examines me. The tech checks my pupil response and asks me questions. After, he tells us that I'll need medical attention if I begin to vomit, develop a headache or lose consciousness; then he declares me fit enough to leave. As he leaves, Detective Bernard comes back in.

When I stand to meet him, James stands with me. He's like a cloak that covers me, but I don't mind. Detective Bernard takes my hand and says, "Please go and get some rest now and I'll see you tomorrow."

"Thank you again, Adrien. We'll see you tomorrow," I answer.

We climb into the back seat of a police car and the officer drives us back to our hotel. During the trip, I lay my head on James' chest and he puts his arms around me. He continues to stroke the hair back from my face and kiss my temple and whisper over and over that I'm safe; he has me. In his arms, I relax more, breathe a sigh of relief and fall into a light sleep. When we arrive at the hotel, we thank the young officer and go inside. James can't seem to keep his hands from me but I like it. I need the reaffirmation of my safety and I've always felt safe with James. We get to our room and I notice we've been moved.

"We're in a different room?" I ask.

James looks at me with concern. "The police needed the other and the hotel was nice enough to put us in this one."

I'm glad, but it adds to a sense of unreality that continues to haunt me. *Except for the ache in your jaw and the split in your lip, Ellen*, I tell myself.

Like a mother hen, James takes me into the bathroom. He runs a hot bubble bath, helps me get undressed and into the water. From the other room, he pours us both a glass of wine. He returns to the bathroom, strips off his clothes and gets in the bath behind me, handing me a glass. His body is big and warm as it surrounds me. We sit in the hot water, sip our wine and allow the warmth to soak away the aches and pains of the day. I rinse my face, wincing at the sting from my lip and allow James to soap and rinse my hair. The shampoo smells wonderful and I relax even more. When the water begins to cool, we get out of the tub. James wraps me in a large luxurious towel. As the tub drains, he leads me into the room and tucks me into bed, kissing my forehead.

"Are you coming to bed?" I ask him sleepily.

"Yes, I'll be right there."

JAMES

James wanders back to the bathroom and picks up their clothes to lay them over the chair in the room. He walks to Ellen and looks to see she's already soundly asleep. As he paces the room, he turns the TV on low and tries to relax, but his mind is so keyed up it won't stop. He pulls a chair to the bed and sits to watch Ellen sleep.

James Russell looks at the woman on the bed. He's glad to get her back. When he met Joe Bell on a routine police call last year he had no idea he would be here, now. The little bastard had double crossed him. He'd kept James hooked with the promise of that damned painting and then sold a clue to its possible location without even consulting him. Then he made plans to leave the area, maybe the country. James hadn't meant to shoot him; he'd just gotten angry when Bell argued with him and insisted he was done with the "Poppy Flowers". James nods and tells himself, *I did what I had to. He was leaving and thought he was done with me, but he was wrong.* After he shot Bell, he'd searched the house, but had found nothing. And then it didn't matter anymore. Fate had given him Ellen. Pretty, intelligent Ellen. She'd come along and he'd known there was something there, known she knew something that would get him to the painting. He sees it now and chuckles out loud thinking about the stupidity of people like Angelo and Maria. Obsessed with a painting, please. He shakes his head in disgust. For James it's all about the money. He already has a viable buyer for the piece. And surprisingly, they really weren't hard to find. The internet is an amazing thing, lots of black market sales going on — if you know where to look. He smiles and relaxes even more. They're back on track. He has Ellen back, a previously unknown competition for the possession of the painting is under arrest, Ellen has no idea she's a tool in his overall plan, and he has an enjoyable companion on his hunt for $55 million dollars. Sighing, he stands and removes his clothes. He'll decide her fate when the painting is in his possession. Maybe he'll keep her for a while longer if she's cooperative. He climbs into bed and pulls Ellen to him. She turns over and snuggles trustingly. He looks down at her with a small smile and a cock of his head as he opens her towel and bends to her to celebrate the end of his day.

17

ELLEN

When I wake in the morning I feel a hundred percent better. The swelling's gone down in my face and lip and I'm starving! I reach my hand out to the bed and feel for James, but he's already up. I begin to smile but then stop when my lip protests. I stretch my aching muscles, muscles that aren't sore from just yesterday's ordeal, but also from James' passion last night. I climb naked out of bed and look around for a note or something as I make my way to the bathroom.

I shut off the shower and hear James' raised voice in the other room. "I grabbed some food from the restaurant downstairs. Hungry?"

I step from the bathroom with a towel wrapped around my body and another one wrapped around my hair. "Starving!" I grin. "Apparently, abduction is good for the appetite." James turns from where he's setting out our meal, takes me into his arms and says, "Don't even joke about that. I was so worried about you and I'm glad to have you here with me."

I wrap my arms around his waist and look up at him, "I'm sorry,

James." Looking around him toward the table I ask. "What do we have for breakfast? What are our plans for the day? We need to see Adrien, don't we?"

James has his arm around me and leads me toward the table. "Yes, I thought we'd eat, you can get ready, and we can see Detective Bernard and then decide where to go from there. Are you up to continuing?"

"Absolutely. I want to see what the cartouche means!"

"Thank you, again, Adrien." I say as I shake his hand. *He's a very good man,* I think. The questions were fairly straightforward; he's even given me back the "Poppy Flowers" information James relinquished before my rescue. "I appreciate all of your help and understanding," I say to him.

"Hopefully, we'll see each other again someday, Ms. Thompson, though under better circumstances." He smiles.

"Yes," I say as I look toward James. "I hope to see you again, too."

It's late morning when we finish at the police station so there's plenty of time to find someone to read the cartouche. We catch a taxi, which drops us off in the downtown area near the obelisk. The shops are open and people are thick on the streets. I'm continuously looking around and behind us with an intensity that's unlike me. Clearly, being abducted has a way of freaking me out.

All around the shopping area are stores which offer items having to do with Egypt and the obelisk. I'm sure someone in any of these establishments can transcribe the papyrus paper, but what if Angelo left a clue somewhere? I don't want to miss anything.

"What do you think, James?"

He shakes his head with a sigh and seems as daunted by this task as I am. Maybe we should take the rest of the day to relax. Maybe we're too tired to think now. I'm turning to him to make this suggestion and I have a spark of inspiration. I dig in my bag and pull out the card from Angelo. The card we got from the fountain in Naples. "What was that poem?" I mutter to myself. James hears me because I now have his full attention.

I look at the picture of the obelisk. Turning it over I read out loud:

Learning is a *Journey,*

It begins as flowers bud,

A Craft is complete with autumn.

Tapping the card on my lip, I walk up the street, thinking. James trails behind me. I stop and reread the card. Journey. Craft. Why are these words italicized? Are they supposed to mean something? Journey? Craft?

I'm deep in thought when a group of businessmen pass by. They're in suits and talking very quickly and animatedly in French. They capture my attention. I shake my head slightly and smile…men….MEN. MEN!!! I catch my breath and look at James. I know my eyes are huge and I'm sure there's a lightbulb above my head.

"What?" he says. "What, Ellen?"

"Men! MEN!!!" I practically scream at him gesturing with my arms.

"Ok. Men. What about them?"

"JOURNEYmen! CRAFTSmen!" With a huge satisfied smile on my face I spin and point. Across and down the street is a large store front with a sign that reads, "THE ARTISAN".

James takes my hand and we jog to the shop. A small bell jingles a welcome. He holds the door open for me and looks left and right before he follows. We cross the threshold and he makes sure the door closes.

"*Bonjour,*" yells a little old man with grey hair from the back of the shop.

"Hello!" I call back to him.

"I'll be right with you."

The proprietor of the shop is not only old and little, but has a quality that reminds me of a garden gnome. I'm taller than average for a woman and the owner looks as if he'll barely reach my shoulder. As we wait for him to come to us, I look around. The shop is full of touristy knick knacks of an Egyptian nature. Due to the proximity to the obelisk, the shop offers a myriad of obelisks for sale: small, large, colored, really anything you can think of. In addition to them, they offer mini sphinx, pyramids, plates, statues and many, many other items. I walk among the wares and look at everything. Toward the back of the shop I spy paintings and pictures, dishes and furniture.

Just then the proprietor comes from the back. "Hello, I am Amun Bahur and I'm the owner of this establishment. How may I help you?" He's dressed in what I think of as traditional Egyptian garb: a loose jacket which hangs down to his knees, belted at the waist with trousers underneath.

"Mr. Bahur. We have an Egyptian cartouche we'd like translated. Would you be able to look at it for us, sir?"

Mr. Bahur studies us for a long moment, long enough I think I'm going to have to ask him again. Then he blinks and nods his head. "Yes, yes. Please come to the back and I'll look at your cartouche." He signals to a young man, turns his back and heads to the rear of his shop, passing through a curtain into a back room. I follow the shop owner. I hear James behind me and as we come through the curtain I'm surprised to see many pieces of art and artifacts, which appear to be authentic, lying about in the back.

Mr. Bahur walks behind a tall work desk, turns and looks at us expectantly.

I pull my bag off, reach in a pocket and pull out the cartouche. I lay it on the table and slide it toward the shop owner.

He studies it without touching and then looks up, first at me and then at James. "Where did you happen to come by the cartouche?"

With a glance at James, I tell Mr. Bahur, "Well Sir, that's quite a long story. I guess it's easiest to say we got it from a friend."

"I'm interested in stories, but let me tell you one. A few years ago a man came into my store. He was interested in Egyptian hieroglyphics and in leaving a message for someone who he was sure would be coming. His message was this item you showed me. The person he was leaving it for was a woman. Are you that woman?"

With a deep breath and a tingle of excitement I say, "Mr. Bahur, I'd like to be completely honest with you, and I hope you'll still help us. I'm not the woman you're speaking of, but I know of her and I know it was Angelo who came to see you."

Mr. Bahur nods his head as if he'd known this and isn't surprised.

"It's been almost five years since I saw Angelo, since he was in my store and asked for my help. There's been no one to inquire about him or what he asked of me in all this time; and now here you are. I'll admit, I'm curious...and I like your face." He smiles a shy smile at me which I return. "I'll look at your drawings and give you what help I'm able."

The shop keeper pulls the paper closer. "As I said, I've seen the papyrus paper drawing before, with Angelo," he says softly. "But it was not complete. And I see you found the cartouche on the obelisk." He takes his time making a decision and then begins...

"The original cartouche shows three Hieros. They're the man, the tree and the obelisk. The three Hieros you found and added are again the tree, the full moon and the scarab." He pushes the papers back.

Was that it? "And do you know what any of that means?"

"When Angelo came to me for help, I hadn't seen him in many years. We knew each other, briefly, in Egypt. He told me the woman would be able to understand the clues that were left for her. You're not that woman so perhaps you're not able to grasp this information."

Perhaps not, I think. This all seems pretty random to me. Man, tree and obelisk? Tree, full moon and bug? I pace back toward James as I think. "Mr. Bahur, if you don't mind me asking, why did you agree to help Angelo? Did he give you any more information? Anything you can share with us?"

He nods his head gently and says, "I will share one other thing with you. It isn't information but more an observation. When he was here, Angelo muttered incessantly about Poppies and Van Gogh. He would stare into space and be unresponsive when spoken to. He would shake his head as if being attacked by bees and talk gibberish. I was concerned for him. He'd grown, unfortunately, gaunt and unstable. The Angelo I knew was an intelligent, caring man. I mourn the loss of him."

I understand the loss of a friend and feel for Mr. Bahur. I listen to him and nod my head in sympathy. Suddenly, I stop, whip around and fix James with a wide eyed expression. "Van Gogh! Of course!

How could I be so dull?"

James walks toward me. "What Ellen? What do you remember?"

I put up one finger so he'll give me a moment and turn back toward Mr. Bahur. "Mr. Bahur, I believe I've solved this part of the puzzle. Do you have any other instruction or thoughts for us? Anything we need from you to continue?"

"Will you tell me what you've discovered?"

I tell both men what I've recalled. "We search for an item that has its origins with Vincent Van Gogh. His obsession with this item is the reason Angelo mutters that name to himself. During the last years of his life, Van Gogh committed himself to a mental asylum at *Saint-Remy* near Arles here in France. While he was there, he painted almost nonstop. Some of his paintings were of the buildings, the staff and many were of the fields. In particular, he became enamored with a stand of cypress trees in a wheat field. I remember learning, when the museum I work for in America came into possession of a Van Gogh painting, that Vincent and his brother were very close; more like best friends than brothers. Vincent and his brother, Theo, wrote often to each other. In one letter, Vincent referred to the cypress trees 'like an Egyptian Obelisk'. I believe the clues on this Egyptian obelisk are meant to take us to Van Gogh's obelisk."

James stands by the table with a look of stunned silence.

Mr. Bahur nods and his face breaks into a huge smile. "Whether you're the woman he expected or not, you are the right woman. You've answered correctly and I do have something for you." He turns away and goes to the back of the room. I look excitedly at James as he steps to me and then I spin back toward Mr. Bahur. He kneels and uncovers the front of a desk with a small safe hidden underneath it. He spins the dial and opens the door. He takes out an item and my heart thumps in my chest. My breath comes rapidly. He locks the safe and comes to me with a small packet. As

I take the packet he offers, I feel elated. "Thank you, Mr. Bahur. Thank you so very much."

"Thank you. I didn't think anyone would ever come for that. I'd like to see what's in it, if you don't mind."

I look over and James nods his agreement. I open the packet. With a downward shake we all watch a single sheet float out.

I pick up the paper; it's a note from Angelo:

Dearest Maria:

You are here. You are reading this so I know you are my one and true love. We are linked in a way others will never understand. Continue on, my love and we will be together again.

Amun doubted you would come, but I knew; I believed! Continue on, my dearest. Follow the cartouche and all will be 'revealed'.

Angelo

"Oh Angelo," I sigh. "Whatever are you doing?" I reach for the papyrus paper and pull it toward me laying it out flat. "The figure, the tree and the obelisk." I look at Mr. Bahur. "The tree, the full moon and the scarab?"

Mr. Bahur nods his head. "Yes, my dear. That's correct."

"Follow the cartouche and all will be 'revealed'," I softly repeat.

I reach into my bag for my phone. I access the internet and search for the cycles of the moon. I'm looking for the date of the full moon.

With a look in James' direction, I say, "The full moon is in two nights. We need to get to *Saint Remy* and the cypresses before then. Thank you again, Mr. Bahur."

He acknowledges me with a nod and a wave as we leave.

I walk out of the back room with James close on my heels. I continue to utilize my phone to access transportation options from Paris to *Saint Remy*. "It looks like the train's going to be our option for getting to the asylum. I'll buy us two tickets on-line for today's departure from *Paris Gare de Lyon*. We've time to get our stuff, get checked out of the hotel and make it to the train station." James nods and flags down a taxi.

18

We enter the *Paris Gare de Lyon* train station and I feel the excitement in my belly. I'm ready to leave Paris and hope my experiences here haven't permanently influenced my love affair with this city. *What would Saint Remy and the asylum bring?* I wonder. *Will we find Angelo, continue with this quest or will it simply fade to nothing? What if the clues stop?*

The train station, with its iconic clock tower, is busy with people traveling in different directions. They speak many languages. As I watch the people I wonder where they're going. What are they doing? Will I ever be back in a normal routine, content in my everyday life? This has been quite an adventure.

James reaches for my hand as the announcement for our train is called over the speaker system.

The trains are all *Train à Grande Vitesse* or TGV Trains. Bullet train is what I've always heard them called. Even though it will take just under four hours to reach *Avignon Centre,* we'll travel almost 430 miles. Once we arrive, we'll take a bus to *St Remy Provence* and the asylum. We'll get there with plenty of time to find somewhere to stay and scope out the surrounding area for cypress trees. Hopefully, there won't be too many trees. The last thing I want to do is wait another month for the full moon.

Because we need to get to *Saint-Paul de Mausole* as quickly as possible, I've purchased inexpensive tickets which put us in a community car. It's relaxing, a bit like the hum of white noise, to hear people talking and only be able to understand parts of it. The countryside passes quickly by and I'm besotted with the beauty of the south of France. There are wheat and sunflower fields, vineyards and quaint villages. It's as if we're passing through a painting or a piece of history. Stunning! Exquisite! Magnificent! My senses can't take it all in and I wish I could stop time and wander the countryside.

Sooner than I would've thought, we pull into the train station. If we had more time, it would be a nice walk as Avignon is a beautiful, quaint town. Our priority, however, is get to the bus and get to *Saint-Paul de Mausole*.

We hail a *Baladine*. Looking at the car, James shakes his head. As an American, I'm sure he's appalled by this funny looking little vehicle. A *Baladine* is a small eco-friendly bright green electric car that they use as taxis when not in service to a group.

It only takes us a few moments to reach the bus station, where the busses leave hourly for *St Remy Provence.* Just as we finish our transaction, we hear the call to board. We climb on a bus filled to capacity. The trip takes under an hour and I feel as if we've just sat when we enter *St Remy Provence*.

Oh my Lord, I think as we walk out of the bus station. *Could this village be any quainter or beautiful?* The buildings are constructed of stone and beautifully detailed. We pass fountains in the parks and centers and ancient restored churches. *I will come back here one day and spend time just being a tourist*, I assure myself.

James gets directions to *Saint-Paul de Mausole*, the asylum where Van Gogh stayed and where he painted his cypress. It's only 20 minutes away if we walk. Stretching our legs after traveling all day will be a welcome activity.

We approach *Saint-Paul de Mausole* where the asylum, which is converted from a monastery, is still a functioning establishment for the treatment of mental disorders. Due to the fame of Vincent Van

Gogh, the asylum offers tours and even has rooms set up as they were in Van Gogh's time — including the set of rooms he utilized while he stayed at *Saint-Paul de Mausole*. That's where I want to be. I want to look out his window and see the location of Van Gogh's cypress tree. As we walk to the building, I notice there are a few different stands of trees, the most conspicuous being a large orchard of olive trees at the entrance, made famous by another painting of Van Gogh's.

Tours run most of the day so there is no wait when we enter the asylum. Within the open areas, we're allowed to roam freely and spend as much or as little time as we desire in each area.

I head up the stairs to the suite of rooms Vincent Van Gogh occupied from 1889 - 1890. The rooms have been preserved and although austere, they're beautiful with their architecture. The monastery depicts a Provencal Romanesque Art that's pleasing to the eye. It's a stone structure with a terra cotta color. There are archways and vine covered walls. It reminds me of a castle with a large bell tower. Outside Van Gogh's window, a field of blooming lavender is a striking contrast to the trees in the distance, which include not only cypress but other evergreens and deciduous broadleaf.

I point out the window. "There! That's where we'll find our tree!"

James steps up behind me to look out the window. "How will we know which one? There must be dozens of trees."

"I'm not sure, but before the full moon rises we need to have found it. If not, we'll be waiting a month for another shot."

I make my way down the hallway to the stairs, where we pass a window. Vibrant color catches my eye. Directly below is an inner courtyard with so many flowering plants I could never count them all. The plants are landscaped in a geometric layout with a walkway. I imagine the monks long ago making their way silently along these places.

The closest accommodations are in *St Remy Provence*. James and I rent a room at the *Canto Cigalo*. The hotel proves to be quaint with most of the rooms decorated in traditional white. There are gardens to walk in and beautiful flowering lavender that fills the air with its sweet, floral scent.

We get comfortable in our room and I say, "You know, James. When this is all over and we're finished with Angelo and the painting, we'll have to travel for pleasure. We've seen so many wonderful places but we haven't been able to truly enjoy them. I want to come back to this area and spend some time."

"I think it's a wonderful idea for you and me to travel back through this area." He looks at me with a small tilt of his head and an introspective look behind his eyes. "There's so much we can learn to do together."

I feel a small shiver chill my blood at the look in his eyes — curious at myself, I give a mental shake figuring it's from lack of sleep and stress. I thread my arms around James' waist to lean into him, resting my cheek against his chest. As his arms come around me, warm and comforting, I forget the foreboding and pull back to look at him with a small smile. James tips his head down and takes my lips with his. He lifts me to straddle his waist with my long legs. As he moves toward the old metal bed he whispers in my ear, "Think we can make the people downstairs blush?"

*****

The next day James and I head back to the asylum. I plan to investigate the stand of trees and look for anything unusual. The second side of the cartouche has a scarab along with the obelisk and the tree so maybe there's something about the beetle that'll come into play.

The weather is lovely and the turtle doves sing back and forth as we make our way to *Saint-Paul de Mausole*. We bypass the main road that goes past the olive orchard and instead make our way around the side and back. As we walk through the fragrant lavender beds I run my hand over the stocks to release their scent. It's heavenly. Soon we're at the forested areas. There appears to be three or four acres of a variety of trees so I hope it won't take us too long to find something of interest.

By late afternoon, I need to rest. I lean against a stone wall and wipe sweat from my brow with the sleeve of my shirt. I pull a bottle of water from my bag and take a long drink. It's warm but satisfying. All optimism aside, we're getting nowhere. There aren't many trees and it's discouraging to make my way through them and come up with nothing but more trees, needles, leaves and sap. Angelo is really beginning to piss me off. If…no, not if, WHEN! When we find him I've half a mind to smack him on the back of his crazy, little head. Across the nearest area of trees I squint and look for James. We separated in an attempt to find something quicker, but that isn't helping. With a flash of color and movement, James heads toward me through the scraggy underbrush. As he nears, he pulls his water bottle from his back pack and stops to take a drink. He recaps the bottle, and looks down with a question on his face. "Anything?" he asks.

"No. No and no and no. Damn it!"

"Well? It's getting late. We still have tomorrow to find something. I think we should head back to the hotel, get something to eat and get ready to come back again early tomorrow."

I sigh. I know he's right but I hate to stop. The sun is dipping and it makes it hard to see clearly among the trees so we're more likely to miss something than to find it. "Ok. You're right. Let's call it a day."

The walk to the hotel feels longer and longer. I'm hot, tired, dirty and hungry. It takes a special effort to lift one foot in front of the other. Only the call of a hot shower and dinner keeps me moving.

As the hotel comes into sight, I breathe a sigh of relief. We order room service from the small on-site café. The proprietor says the meal will be delivered to our room in 40-60 minutes so we have plenty of time to get cleaned up and relax. "Could you send a bottle of Cabernet Sauvignon with our dinner?" James asks.

"*Oui, Monsieur.*"

When we get to our room, I sit hard and flop backward to lay sprawled out on the bedspread. James laughs and straddles my knees. "Come on, kiddo," he says and helps me sit up as he pulls my shirt off over my head. "You and me are gonna use up all the hot water in this here establishment."

I chuckle and as he steps backward I reach down to pull off my boots. James steps back and runs his hand down my spine causing me to shiver. He unsnaps my bra allowing it to fall over my shoulders and land on my lap. I give him a wicked smile as I grab his belt buckle and pull him forward. I unbuckled his belt and decide that I'm really not all that tired.

*****

Spent passion, great food and a good night's sleep are magic in the promotion of a reinvigorated mood and commitment to our goal. I feel great as we retrace our steps to the asylum and the stand of cypress. *Today will be the day!* I think. The full moon is tonight and I'm confident we'll find what we need.

We walk around the building and through the lavender fields. I study the approaching forest. A wall runs between the fields and the trees and there are a couple of buildings within easy access to the forest. Maybe Angelo hid "Poppy Flowers" in one of the out buildings? By his correspondence, it's obvious he's becoming less and less aware of not only his current situation, but also his past. How long can he run? How long before we find him sitting in a puddle somewhere? His paranoia and lunacy are escalating. He has to wear out soon.

We split up again as we enter the cool shade of the trees. Today, I not only look at the cypress and their surrounding area but at the man-made structures and how they correlate to the trees. I notice a run of cypress mirrors the rock wall and the wall mirrors, in a lesser way, the buildings beyond. Of all the trees, these are the most uniform. I move within them and look toward the east where the full moon will rise and keep the wall and buildings at my back. Almost as an afterthought, I feel the crown of my head pinging. *What is it? What's here?* I move down the line of cypress trees looking each over with a fine tooth comb. A dozen trees in, I think I see a glint about 10 feet up the tree. I look it over. Each tree is tall and healthy, a dark green with densely packed branches and needles. They're large and tall, but I really don't think they'll bear my weight and climbing one of them doesn't look to be easy. "James!" I yell. "James can you come here?"

"What is it?" he asks as he comes through the trees.

"I think I may have found something different on this tree, but I'm not tall enough to see. Do you think I can get on your shoulders? Can you hold me?"

He gives me a look of arrogant amazement that has me laughing. "I didn't mean to question your masculinity, kind sir."

He pulls me into his arms to give me a playful shake. "Climb on, Baby! Let's go for a ride." With that he stoops down and I swing a leg over his shoulders. Easily, he stands with me balanced on his shoulders, my feet and legs wrapped under his arms and around his waist. He walks forward and I see where an area was cleared and there's a wedge hacked into the tree. The smell of pine is intense and I notice where the sap ran and dried once the surgery was complete.

Directly over the wound is a metal scarab that reflects the bright sunlight.

James and I sit at the base of the tree.

"When the moon rises, it'll take until just after midnight before the light directly hits the area cut out of the tree. We need to be here to see what'll happen when these factors come together." I say.

"It's midafternoon and we have twelve hours to wait. Why don't we head back to town and get some food and relax? We can check our packs and make sure we're prepared for anything that might happen."

When we walk into *St. Remy* it's relaxing to wander up and down the streets, looking at shops and cafes. In one square my eye catches what appears to be white, plastic bags all strung together in a line. As they blow in the wind they appear to be dancing. "Let's eat here, James. I love how whimsical it looks."

We head to the café, which is called *Café Les Filles du Patissier* or Daughters of the Pastry Chef, and take a seat beneath a white canopy. I'm curious and slide my chair back to look at the bags. They're hung in rows a few feet above the area and as the wind blows, they move gently to and fro making a subtle crinkly noise that's surprisingly pleasant. I ask our waiter, "What're the bags for?"

The waiter glances upward and explains that they're called 'The Canopies' and are an inspiration of the artist Jacques Salles. They'll be on display for a limited time so he's glad we have the opportunity to enjoy them.

"So am I," I reply. "How unique."

Just as I'm going to place an order for a glass of wine, the waiter is gone. I glance toward James, "Where did he go?"

He shakes his head. "Not sure. Pretty quick little guy. Here one minute and gone the next."

Although it takes the waiter about 20 minutes to make another appearance we don't mind. It's a beautiful day to relax in this lovely square in France. When the waiter comes around again, we order wine, peach fig salads with mozzarella, piston vegetable soup and tartine bread. The wine comes and we watch people as we sip. The plan is simple. We'll be at the tree before the moon rises, and we'll stay there throughout the night. *Best to go back to the hotel and get some rest,* I think. After what would be considered too long a wait in America, our lunches show up. The food is wonderful and the wine is heady. All in all, it's a lovely afternoon, slow and relaxing — just what we both need.

At *Canto Cigalo,* I run a list of all necessary items through my head. I plan on checking to make sure I have everything we'll need for tonight's excursion. Flashlight, matches, Leatherman tool, the stone suncross that's one of the items we found in the fountain in Naples, paper, pencil and the key I removed from Joe Bell's hand. I used the key from the music box but I still don't know where this one goes and have carried it with me all this way. It would be a shame to need it tonight and not have it ready.

Later we're fed and rested. We step into the twilight of evening and head in the direction of *Saint-Paul de Mausole*. It'll be closed when we arrive and we hope we won't come in contact with anyone, employees or locals.

We decide not to use additional light to traverse our way to the stand of trees. It's not fully dark yet and we've walked the ground quite a few times. We agree it should be okay and will draw less attention to us if we can do it without extra light. We veer off to walk between the many types of trees and underbrush. A nightingale calls in the distance, singing forlornly to attract his mate. The bird's song adds a touch of melancholy to an evening of adventure.

We near the tree, then stand and watch as if we expect it to break from the ground with a song and dance.

As the moon rises, it becomes brighter and brighter; it's a flashlight in the sky. I can't stand still as the shadows within the tree move and shift with the light of the moon. The entire area is illuminated but with the curve of the trunk the moon will need to rise to a greater height before it passes through the notched wound. I pace back and forth and back and forth. I continue to watch the moon impatiently, as if my desire will move it more quickly across the night sky.

When James says my name, I stop pacing. He glances at the tree. I look from his face upward to see the moonlight shine through the juncture of the tree and come into contact with the metal scarab. As the moon rises higher, somehow the light intensifies into a narrow beam. I don't know how this happens, but I witness it. The beam moves across the ground and up the stone wall. Walking slowly, we trail behind it and wait to see what, if anything will happen. The beam of light clears the stone wall and falls upon an outbuilding a few feet away. When the light hits the building about midway up, a radiance blasts forth. We step back and involuntarily cover our eyes. Quicker to recover, I slide over the stone wall and approach the area where the moonlight shines so bright. Hesitantly, I slide my hand into the beam, almost afraid it may burn. The light reflects on my palm as I move my hand in and out of it. James stands near me and I turn to assess what thoughts he may have but he doesn't say anything; just watches me. I study the wall and make out a faint outline that resembles the stone circle, the suncross I got from the fountain. In an attempt to see better, I move in front of the moonbeam. When the shadow of my body blocks the light, the outline I'm seeking disappears, only to reappear when I step out of the beam. I step back and drop my bag, rummaging through it until I pull out the suncross. I make sure to stay out of the way of the light and place the suncross over the outline created on the wall and push. Without warning, the ground under my feet collapses and I find myself on one knee looking up at James' startled face as a trap door swings shut and I'm locked in an underground chamber.

19

When the trapdoor swings shut I'm plunged into complete darkness. In this stygian black I swear out loud with the knowledge that I've left my bag, with my flashlight, lying on the ground next to the building. *Nothing like being completely prepared, huh Ellen?* I berate myself. Standing, I reach out a tentative hand and feel for the wall. With surprise I feel an immediate dizziness. I attribute this to the lack of stimuli: there's no sound, no light and the only smell is of the earth. I inch my foot forward, making sure the ground is solid before I move my body. I'm sure I moved toward what should be a side wall, but begin to question my decision when after some time I don't come into contact with anything. I stop where I am and tilt my head back to yell.

"JAMES!"

There's nothing. *Really, how insulated could this hole be? Can he hear me?* I yell again, louder. "JAMES!" I listen but the only thing I hear is my own breathing, breathing that's beginning to sound panicked, and the heavy sound of my heart.

"Damn it," I sigh. "Ok, El. What are you going to do to get out of this one?" I decide, to stay in one place is folly, so I begin the painful process of inching a foot forward, assuring the ground is stable, and moving my body into that spot. I repeat this over and over and have yet to encounter a wall. Beads of sweat run down the sides of my face, between my breasts and down the small of my back. *Where in the hell am I? How long can this cavern go on?*

Moments later, I glance around and realize the darkness isn't as complete. I can't see, can't make out any shapes but my senses register a lightening. Excited, I continue with my tedious process of moving forward. Still there's no sound, not even a promise of a sound. Before long I make out blackness on either side of me, about eight feet away. My heart jolts in fear before I identify the walls of the corridor. I move to the right and reach to touch the wall, it's dirt - dry and crumbly. I tell myself to not get excited and end up in a worse situation, to proceed slowly and carefully. Still moving slowly, but with my hand running on the wall, I move inexplicitly forward.

A bit later I'm able to hear voices. They're very low, hums sounding like a faraway engine but with the lack of other sounds they seem almost loud. I move forward, ever forward and the hum grows louder. Now I can make out each voice. They come to me like a chant. An invocation. *What the hell? Where am I and what's going on?* Seeing the tunnel make a turn, I lean forward to try and make out anything down the next branch. Ahead of me is a set of stairs carved out of the earth. They're reinforced with large slabs of rock. I look around but other than the muted voices, there's nothing to indicate I'm not alone. I take a deep breath and let it out slowly to defuse the nerves riding hard on me. I figure moving forward is really my only option so I turn the corner and start for the stairs.

At the head of the stairs there's a small hallway with a door at the end. The door is plain and in the partial light, appears to be old and unmaintained. The fit of the door is loose and light filters around the edges. The voices come from behind this door. *Ah, man,* I think. *This is not what I thought I'd be doing when we started out tonight.*

I step to the door. I wish I could see through the cracks on either side, but they're not big enough to allow me to peek. Laying my hands flat on the door, I lean in and study it closely. The latch is dated and rusty. It's a simple mechanism — lift and it opens. The door appears to open into the room beyond. *So? Lift and push?* I wonder whether it will squeak if I open it a crack. Can I eavesdrop on what's happening beyond? *Well, El. You can't stay here forever.*

With a lift of the latch and a gentle push the door swings on its hinges. It doesn't squeak, which I'm thankful for, but it doesn't open very far either. It's a heavy door and is going to take a good push to get it open enough for me to enter the room. *Here goes nothing...* I lean into the door and give it a push, all the while trying to control its swing. Slipping around the door, I lean back into it and push it shut. The room beyond is lit with a faint, defused light produced by candles. The chanting is louder now and very distinct. The words are French. It sounds familiar, like stepping into a church, but still foreign. I'm in an alcove and I'm unable to see into the room ahead. I'll need to step forward, into the light and around the wall. I move forward silently and peer around the edge of the barrier.

In front of me is a large, oblong room. There appears to be some sort of ritual taking place. Perhaps 25 people surround a makeshift altar. On the altar a person lays silently. It's unclear whether the body is alive or dead. There's no movement, no breath I can discern and although every few moments one of the chanters pours water on him, there's no reaction.

All the participants are dressed in robes of pale colors, though the robes aren't identical in style. Some are formal, some gothic. Most of the people gathered are women but there are three or four men. In the hope of finding an exit, I step further into the room and a couple of people on the outer fringe see me. I stop with wide eyes and hold my breath but they show no reaction and turn back to the ritual. I can't understand the words but with the look of the body I wonder if it's the last rites.

I study the room. There are two additional doors, hopefully one of them leads to an exit. There are no windows on this level but the ceiling is two or three stories above and there are small windows at the top. Windows, that even during the day, would let in very little natural light. The walls themselves are constructed of stone and the room has a definite chill.

I make my way around the outside of the participants, keeping my back to the walls and move toward one of the doors. With a flourish and a rising of voices the ceremony ends.

Beginning at the altar and moving toward me, each person turns and stares at me. My scalp breaks out in a sweat and a shiver runs down my spine. *Damn*, I think. *Freaky.* As the people part, one of the women approaches me. The robe she wears has a symbol stitched onto it. The symbol resembles the suncross I used to trigger the trap door, but it's more ornate. The spokes are broader and have three points at the far ends. The circle surrounding the cross is made of dots.

"Qui etes-vous?" The woman says. *"Pourquoi es-tu ici?"*

"I'm sorry. I don't speak French," I say with a small shake of my head.

"You are American?" The woman raises an eyebrow, cocks her head and looks at me.

"Yes."

"Why are you here?"

"I'm sorry to intrude. I accidentally ended up outside this door and didn't know where else to go."

"There's only one entrance on the other side of that door and it requires a special key. I don't believe it was an accident you arrived here." Tipping her head a little the woman asks, "How did you come by the key?" She stands still as she asks her questions. It's eerily quiet considering there are so many people present.

"I followed clues left by an acquaintance. The clues led me to you and to the wall outside. I didn't know the key would lead me here." After a pause, I ask, "Do you know Angelo?" I figure it can't hurt to be direct.

"Nous avons fini." The woman says quietly and the assembled

people begin to filter out. Two of the men stop and help the man off the altar and out the door. She says, "Come with me."

I follow down a long corridor. The building is lit with candles and the temperature begins to warm noticeably. As we pass through another door, the interior of the building becomes more modern. Electric light fills a hallway floored with tile and finished with painted walls covered with artwork. The woman leads me into a study and indicates for me to take a seat. She sits across from me and studies me.

"A few years ago, a man came to us. He felt he was near the end of his mortal life. He asked for the "Consolamentum" to remove his sin so he might move to the next level. We're profoundly honored to help all in their quest for purity. We thought this man would stay with us for the short duration of his physical life, but after speaking privately with one of the Prefects, he disappeared. We've not heard from him since."

So Angelo is dying? "Do you know what he's dying from? May I speak with the Prefect whom he spoke privately with? I'm hoping Angelo may have left something with him."

"I'm not a medical doctor but he appeared to simply be wasting away. As for the Prefect, you will have to hurry. He's the man you just witnessed the "Consolamentum" performed for."

I follow the Priestess into another room further down the main hallway. It's a bedroom and in the center of the bed lies the man I saw in the main chamber. If possible, he appears to have shrunken more in the short time since his rite. The Priestess approaches him and speaks in a gentle voice.

"Bons Hommes."

He opens his eyes and looks at her with adoration.

"Brother, this woman is in search of information about Angelo. Will you help?"

The old man looks from the Priestess to me. He opens and closes his mouth a few times but no sounds come out. When he lifts his emaciated hand toward the leader, she takes it and sits on the bed beside him. She leans in to better hear him. The Priestess nods her head as it rests next to his face and sitting up, she pats his hand, releases it and stands.

"Brother Giles told me where the belongings Angelo left with him are." She walks to the dresser across the room and opens the top drawer, reaches in to retrieve a packet.

I look at the packet and feel like a starving man viewing a table of food. I want to jump her and wrench it from her grip! Instead, I wait to see what she'll do.

"Sister," she says to me, "let's give Brother Giles his privacy and step back into the study." She moves through the door and down the hallway. I have no choice but to follow.

When we arrive back in the study, I'm surprised to see James pacing the room. "Ellen!" he yells and rushes toward me. "Are you all right?" He grabs me and gripping my arms tightly, he looks me over.

"I'm fine, James. I'm fine." I glance at the woman with a question.

With a small smile the woman says, "We found him as he wandered the perimeter of the building yelling for you. We thought it better to bring him in before someone contacted the authorities."

I give a little bark of laughter and turn to hug James with a quick, tight clench. "James, we found what Angelo left."

The Priestess holds the packet for me to take. "Thank you for your help." I give a small smile and nod. With the packet in hand, I walk to the couch and take a seat. James sits beside me.

The first item is a photo. It's a candid shot of a middle aged man and woman standing in front of a majestic three story building. They have their arms wrapped around each other and they're smiling. Slightly behind them and off to one side is a statue. They're both dark skinned with dark hair and the woman is strikingly beautiful. They look happy. Turning over the photo I read an inscription:

Angelo and Maria 2010
Mohamed Mahmoud Khalil Museum, Cairo Egypt

And written in a bold, shaky hand beneath was:

"I sometimes think I am really continuing that man."

"Yep," I say as I hand the photo to James, "that's Maria all right."

James takes the photo and looks it over. "Do you have any idea what the quote means?"

"Absolutely not." I say with conviction. "Let's see what else there is, shall we?"

The next item proves to be a missive from Angelo. Something we've come to expect but this one is different.

I am soon to die. I know that now and I welcome the silence that will come with the darkness of death. Finally, I will know some measure of peace. Peace from the 'Poppies'.

I will take my sin to its initiator and I will be done.

I am finished...

I read the note out loud to James. I almost feel sorry for Angelo. "I don't know where we go from here."

"Ahem..." With surprise, I turn to the Priestess. I had almost forgotten she was in the room, she's so quiet. "I may be able to help with that."

The Priestess walks to me. "I can identify the quote you just read. May I see the photo?" she asks, reaching her hand out. I hand the photo to her. She turns it over. "Yes, I know this quote. It was from Vincent Van Gogh regarding Adolphe Monticelli, the French painter. Van Gogh adopted the use of color after witnessing Monticelli's painting in France."

Um? I think. *How in the hell does she know that? What a random bit of information...*

"How do you know this?" James asks.

"I'm a French woman." With a smile she adds. "And I instruct school children in history and Adolphe Monticelli is a famous local person. He lived close to here — in Marseille. In fact, his family still resides there. They run a museum dedicated to his work."

I look at James with resignation. "Looks like we're going to Marseille. Maybe we can meet with one of the Monticelli and see if Angelo contacted them."

20

Getting comfortable in our cabin on the train doesn't prove to be a problem. We stow our bags, hang up coats and lay down on the bed to cuddle. James turns on his back and I drape over his front with my hands on his chest to support my chin.

"Tell me about your childhood, James. I want to know everything about you."

JAMES

As he looks at her, James knows no one wants the specifics about his childhood and he, in particular, doesn't want to relive most of it. Instead of the truth, he spins a story he thinks she'll like. A story of a beloved adopted child brought to a privileged upbringing in a true nuclear family. The story emerges from a fantasy world that includes an indulgent father and mother, with a spoiled desired son. In truth, his birth mother was an addict and mostly nonexistent. Shortly after his involvement in the death of a neighborhood boy, James was tossed into the foster system like a piece of human waste and only as a teenager did he get placed with a family — the woman who he refers to as his mother to people who know him; but even she doesn't truly know him or care for him. To his parents, he's the charity case that makes them look good to their society crowd.

James puts his hands behind his head and looks at the ceiling. He allows his imagination to roam free. He talks about fishing with his father, birthdays with a large extended family and holidays that would rival most. James grins at his creations. He talks of a love of working with his hands that his father has given him and the many projects they complete together, the pride in a job well-done.

"What kind of projects do you like to do best?" Ellen asks, rapt with attention at his words.

James looks up with a thought and says, "Wood. My father always loved wood and I got that from him. The feel and smell of it, like a living being. Warm, not like metals which are cold. Wood, I think, wood is my favorite."

"Do you have a special piece? Do you have any of them in your home?" she prompts.

"My father and I worked on so many that I have no favorite." He continues to embellish as he warms to his story. "I saw one a few days ago, though, one I would love to get my hands on." He looks down at her and then back up, remembering. "The bureau in Joe Bell's living room was old, but wonderful; so stately."

ELLEN

My smile slowly melts off my face as the realization of what he's just said sinks in. I see he's still talking, can feel him breathe, but the roar in my ears drowns out the sound of his voice. I tip my head to lay it on his chest and stare into the room to try to calm my breath and the heavy beat of my heart. I must have heard him wrong. That was it! I'm sure I heard him incorrectly. I roll off James' chest and stand next to the bed with my back to him. Snippets of his conversation are coming to me, off and on; they are bubbles rising and bursting from a pool of water.

"I would pull the drawers and sand them until they're back to their original luster. You and I could select just the right sealant or stain. It would be perfect in a proper room…"

I'm thinking, thinking back to those days in Joe Bell's house. I'd noticed the bureau; it caught my eye when I was first there and purchased the mirror. But when I went back and found him dead, the day I called the police, James' supposed first time in the house, it was destroyed. There was no beautiful old bureau. When had he seen it? When had he been in Joe Bell's house before I called? Why would he be there? *You must have misunderstood him, right*? I step a few paces away and turn to face James on the bed. I look at him, try to concentrate, to hear and understand what he's saying.

James quiets as he realizes I'm standing still and staring at him. I'm sure my face is pale and my eyes wide with shock. He spins to sit on the bed with his feet on the floor and his elbows on his knees as he eyes me and gives me a smile, a sly smile.

"Oops. Guess I let the cat out of the bag, huh Ellen?" He chuckles softly. "Well? It was just a matter of time, you're a smart girl. You would've known at some point, right?"

As I stand across the cabin from James, I go completely still. I can't even breathe. *What's he saying? What's happening?*

James stands and approaches me. He puts his arms around me. "Ah pretty Ellen. Such a willing partner you were. You gave me all you have." He leans down to look into my stunned face. "And I do mean ALL, right Baby?"

Oh my God, I think. I push against him and mutter. "I don't understand. When did you see the bureau in Joe Bell's house? Were you there before the day I called the police?"

James wraps his arms around me and begins to rock me back and forth. "Ellen, Ellen, Ellen. You don't know how long I've wanted to tell you everything. That crazy Joe Bell, he planned to double cross me. He was going to pull out of everything. I couldn't let him do that; you understand, right?" He pulls back and tips my head up to look into my face. He gives me a small kiss on the lips as he continues in his tirade of crazy.

"Now it's you and me baby. We'll find the painting, sell it and live like royalty. Nothing and no one will come between us."

Violently, I give James a shove and push back from him. "I think I'm going to be sick," I mutter softly. I thought I LOVED this man. I thought he loved me, but I'm fast realizing I don't even know who he really is. I feel dirty, want to scrub myself clean. I pace as far as I can in the small room and stand with my back to him as I try to think.

"Come on, El," he cajoles. "You play your cards right and we can continue as we are: you and me, together."

With my back still to him I intone, "I'm not going or doing anything with you."

Chuckling at me, he says, "Don't start being stupid now, Baby."

I spin back to face him and shout, "Don't call me baby! I'm not your baby! I don't even know who you are."

"Well see, the problem we have here, El," he says quietly as he advances on me and becomes more and more threatening with each step, "is that if you're not with me, you're against me."

With survival my only thought, I swing my fist and catch him in the throat. Completely unprepared, James bends and grabs his neck, choking. I wrench open the cabin door and bolt. I don't even know where I'm going — I'm on a train, for God's sake, but have to move.

James recovers quicker than I anticipated and I hear a bellowed, "ELLEN!" behind me.

I head toward the rear of the train, running. I don't know if he sees which direction I take. Unfortunately, my escape on a train is a straight shot with very few places to hide. I just need a moment, a moment to breathe. *James*, I think. *My James not only didn't exist any longer, he never did. I've been played.*

I move through the train and I can't hear the sound of pursuit behind me. Maybe I've gotten lucky and James has gone toward the front, away from me. I don't know how much that will benefit me, but at this point I'm willing to take anything I can get.

"A weapon. I need a weapon." I'm repeating this like a litany. A chant. A prayer. He's bigger and faster, but I'll be smarter. I square my jaw and set my attention to survive this hour, this day.

I slow my escape and watch for something that will be of use. When I pass what appears to be a Porters room, I stop. I try the knob and am relieved when the door opens. I close the door behind me, lean back against it and take my first good deep breath since I fled the cabin. The room is completely dark and I grope the wall looking for a light switch. I click it on to realize I'm in a mini-galley. There's tableware, utensils and serving aids as well as sheets, pillows and the like. I have to be able to find something here. I rummage through the drawers and cupboards and find a couple of carving knives. I slide them into the back of my belt and continue to search. Suddenly I freeze. What sounds like a large body is coming down the aisle.

"E-l-l-e-n." His sing-song voice gives me chills. I still myself and strain to hear him. "You do know you're on a train, right? There's nowhere to go, baby." His voice fades as he moves down the aisle. I sigh and relax.

Gotta make a plan, El, I tell myself. *You aren't going to continue to be that lucky. He'll be back and he's right — there's nowhere to go on this train.* Three hours to Marseille and we'd been on the train about 40 minutes when James revealed himself. Can I hold out two more hours? And then what? What will I do once we get to

Marseille?

I continue to search the room.

JAMES

When Ellen hits James, he can't believe it. Doubled over and coughing, he struggles to get his breath back as he watches her open the door and run. *Bitch!* he thinks. As he massages his throat, he straightens and heads after her. "ELLEN!" he yells. He'll teach her a thing or two about messing with him. It'll be worse than the beating he gave Joe Bell and way worse than the paltry hits she'd taken in Paris. She'll learn! Oh yeah, she'll learn — and then, when his anger is satisfied, he'd dispose of her and go on his own.

When James gets to the head of the train, he stops and looks around. Where did she go? Where can you hide on a train? He becomes angrier and angrier as Ellen continues to elude him. Instead of shame, James' anger has always been a sense of pride; something that makes him different, strong.

JAMES 32 Years Ago...

"Jamie, Jamie!" the group of boys call his name. James hates it when they do that. He hates the need to run and hide, but that's what he does. At eight years of age, James is smaller than the other boys and they constantly pick on him and remind him he's inferior — that his mother's not married and he's a "little bastard." He'd heard the adults in the neighborhood call him that, too, and worse things about his mother. Even at eight, he knows his mother is weak. She never protects him like a mom is supposed to.

"Jamie! Jamie!" they call. James holds completely still in his hiding spot among the garbage cans in the alley. He's sure they won't find him here. He still hasn't completely healed from the last time they caught him in the open, with nowhere to go and nowhere to hide. He breathes deeply in an attempt to be as silent as possible and strains his ears to listen for their footsteps. Maybe if they pass him by he can sneak out and run home to hide in his room. At least he'll be safe for another day.

When he hears nothing, he leans from the cans and looks around. Nothing. No sounds except the wind howling down the alley bringing the smell of old garbage. James crawls from among the cans and spilled waste. He begins to walk slowly toward the end of the alley. He listens and watches with every step.

All of a sudden, a teenage boy steps into the mouth of the alley. "There you are, little bastard!" James freezes and steps back further into the alley. Can he outrun this boy? He's smaller and not as strong, but he's desperate. "Where you goin'?" the boy calls out. As James prepares to run there's a noise behind him. He spins around and sees three boys coming from the other direction. Panic roars into his body and he spins back to the single boy. Only there isn't a single boy there any longer. At the end of the alley are multiple boys. James knows this isn't going to end well. The blood pounds so loud in his head he can't hear the names as they close him in. When they get close, they push him back and forth to each other. They yell and slap him when he falls into them. As he begins to cry the slapping turns to punching and kicking. One of the boys, one of the leaders, grabs him and pushes him to the ground. He sits on James and begins to punch him mercilessly in his face and on his chest. The pain is blinding and James thinks he's going to black out as a fog covers his vision. Suddenly, the fog begins to change to red. His body begins to heat in the most wonderful way and his vision is no longer cloudy – it's crystal clear and like a big long tunnel. James reaches up to the boy who sits on his chest and grabs his throat with a small claw of a hand and squeezes. He feels he has the strength of a hundred men and for a moment, he wonders if he's a super hero just being born.

The boy gags and pulls at James' hand, but it doesn't do him any good. James hangs on and begins to sit up, begins to drive the older boy backwards. The other boys have fallen silent and back up a few steps. They stand and peer at each other as the strange turn of events occurs before them.

As James digs his fingers into the boy's throat, he feels invincible. He pushes the boy onto his back and crawls on him. He sits on the boy's chest as that boy once sat on James. He looks down on the boy with a gleam in his eyes and applies as much pressure as he can. He feels pieces of the throat give way. The boy emits a small gurgle and his eyes dull. The hands that flailed at James drop to the concrete and then he is still, completely still. As James looks at the boy, he feels no remorse, no sorrow; all he feels is satisfaction and a growing bud of glee. Never again will this boy beat him. Never again will James have to worry and run from this tormentor. James hears the other boys as they shift and begin to whisper among themselves. He realizes even though this boy is gone, there are many more to deal with. James stares at them and around the circle. He slowly stands up, legs straddling the body of the dead boy. Something in his face must have terrified the gang because they all turn and flee the alley; yelling like the devil himself is chasing them.

As James thinks back to this time of awaking, he smiles. Over the years, he's allowed his anger, his beast within, to take over and to handle things for him. He's never regretted it and knows it will all turn out for the best. He knows he is a special being. When, in his anger, he'd beaten and killed Joe Bell, for just the smallest of moments he looked at the body and wondered what he had done and what he was going to do. All through the next day he second guessed his actions. Joe Bell was his link to the location of the "Poppy Flowers", or so he thought. Then, just like a gift, the call of a dead body at the Bell residence came in. His partner, Boyd hadn't wanted to take the call. "Let a uniform get it," he said, but James insisted. He had to see what happened, had to follow the case closely; and what's closer than the investigating detective? And with the elimination of Joe Bell, fate gave him Ellen. Sweet Ellen who is soon to die, also; but he isn't worried. Everything in his life, from the day in the alley, has turned out. He's learned to turn himself over to the monster inside and it's all taken care of. Now he just had to find the Bitch.

ELLEN

I salvage all I can from the galley, open the door, and peek up and down the hallway. The train's moving at top speed now, a straight shot for Marseille. As I walk down the hallway I'm sent in a back and forth motion, occasionally bouncing off walls and doors. Every few minutes, my heart jumps and I reach for one of my hidden knives when an innocent passenger enters the car and passes me in the hall.

Because I fled the cabin so quickly, I've left my bag with my cell phone. *Should I chance going back for it?* The thought that overrides all others is to call the police, in particular Adrien Bernard, for help. I have his number programmed into my phone from the first night. I feel deeply he's a good cop, that I can trust him. Of course, I thought the same thing about James just an hour ago so I don't know if I can trust my own judgment.

Since James passed the galley and continued on toward the front of the train, I decide it's worth it to head in the direction of our cabin. I'll keep an eye and ear out for him and get my phone. With it, I'll find a safe place to hide before calling Adrien.

I make my way back the way I'd come and see a group of young people who are obviously in the middle of a party. They're loud and jovial and I flatten myself against the wall as they near. My attention is so focused on them I don't notice the large man enter the car, but he notices me.

"ELLEN!" he yells.

At his bellow, I spin and block the hallway with my body. The group of people slow as they collide with me. My adrenaline spikes and I'm in a panic as I begin to push my way through the group. I can feel James bearing down on me. I push more and more frantically to clear my way.

"Hey lady," one of the men complains as I shove them back, but being polite is the least of my concerns.

"ELLEN!" I hear James shout again. I feel as if a steam roller is about to run me over as he nears. I pull a knife from my belt and swing to face the threat. Dizziness almost overcomes me when I look into his face. He wears a maniacal smile of triumph and although he bears the trappings of James, I know this is a stranger to me — a man I've never met.

People in the crowd see my knife and with cries of alarm they fall back allowing James quicker access. He reaches for me and I swing with the knife. I aim for anything vital but he easily bats my arm aside and grabs my wrist. He squeezes so hard I'm sure my bones will break. He twists and I drop the knife. I look into his face and know I'm done. He'll kill me here, in the hall, surrounded by panicked, innocent onlookers.

JAMES

When James comes out of the train car to head to their cabin, he's furious. He's been to the front of the train and now has worked his way slowly back in an attempt to find Ellen's hiding place. As he closes the door from one car to the next, he hears a large group coming down the hall. He turns fully and catches sight of Ellen as she makes her way through the throng of people. Satisfaction and a blood lust crash into him and he begins to run down the aisle.

"ELLEN!" he shouts out like a battle cry. When she turns with a look of pure panic it spurs him on. James picks up his pace as she pushes people out of her way. He bellows her name again just because he can and because he knows it'll increase her fright.

"ELLEN!" He laughs in delight as she pulls a knife from her belt and stands to face him. He admires her desire to win, but there's no way that will happen. He moves into her. He fetes when she swings the weapon and bats her hand away. He grabs her wrist, squeezes and twists. As the knife drops and she looks at him, he knows what a hound must feel when the scented is chased to ground. How sweet she is. He'll have to do this again. Not just kill, but killing with the chase. It's so much better. As he looks down at her and imagines her dead by his hand, he feels himself harden in his pants. The monster is definitely loose.

ELLEN

As people scatter in both directions my sense of self-preservation drains away, then just as quickly surges back stronger than ever. James leers down at me with a sick, lustful gaze that makes the bile rise in my throat. He yanks me with a wrist that's numb and yet somehow screams in pain. I gasp and fall into his chest as he wraps his arms around me.

"Now, Ellen. Where did you find your little sticker? That's not very nice, is it Baby?" He spins me with my back to his front and gazes down between us. He pulls the second knife out of my waist band. "You're just full of surprises, aren't you? Maybe I'll use one of these on you, huh? How would you like that?" He's rubbing himself on me and I begin to thrash about and throw my head and feet back at him. James tosses the knife down the hallway and spins me back around and into the wall. He grabs me by the neck. With pressure on my neck he begins to lift me up the wall. I rip at his hand with my nails and feel just my toes touch the ground. I can't get any air to breath. *Don't panic, El, don't panic, El,* I repeat to myself but it's hard as my eyesight begins to fade and I see stars.

From both sides of the car security guards enter and yell for us to stop. I don't know much about French security but I'm sure I'll be dead before they drag him off me.

Triumph flares in James' eyes as my arms drop to my sides. I slide my hand to the front waistband of my jeans and feel the corkscrew from the galley. I act compliant and beaten as I grasp the corkscrew handle. I hold it with the metal screw sticking out between my fingers. With a tear at my heart for the man I thought he was, I punch up with all my might and will and drive the corkscrew into James' throat until my fingers hit. With a wretched cry, I twist it sharply and pull it out bringing skin, tendons and blood.

James grasps his throat with a shocked expression. He stumbles backwards — down the aisle and against a wall. Bending over holding my own throat, I cough and attempt to catch my breath. I stare at James with terror and horror. Blood spurts between his fingers. He's covered in his life's blood and so am I. As he collapses against the wall and slides to the floor, the security rush us. They grab me and shove me into the wall. They take the corkscrew from my numb fingers, zip tie my hands behind me and lead me down the hall. As I look back, I see a group of men standing over James' prone body. His eyes are open and glazed, his hands still grip his throat.

21

The security officers walk me into a private compartment and forcibly sit me down on a berth. I'm in shock and chilled, my teeth chattering visibly. Although my throat feels as if I've swallowed glass and my voice comes out strained and raspy, I ask, "Detective Adrien Bernard. Could someone call Detective Adrien Bernard of the National Police in Paris? Please, his number's in my phone in my cabin. I need you to call him."

The officers gaze at each other. The one in charge nods to the other officer. He leaves the compartment and I hope he's going to get my phone or at least make the call.

"Can you tell me what's going on?" I ask for what feels like the hundredth time. "Is he dead? Are you sure he's dead? Please, can you give me any information?" With a deep sigh I clear my throat and change tactics. "Has Detective Bernard been contacted?" The officer is stone-faced. This has been going on for a half-hour. I'm calming, but really want to know if James is dead. By my estimations, we'll arrive in Marseille soon and I don't know what to expect. My probable killing of James was totally self-defense, but how does that work in France? I need to quit scaring myself, so I lay my head against the window pane and try to make my mind blank.

With my hands cuffed behind me I'm unable to truly get comfortable, but this will have to do.

When the train's speed changes, I lift my head and watch the officer. He opens the door and speaks to someone in the hall. I lean forward and strain to hear but can't make out what they say. After he closes the door, the officer sits to resume his vigil. With a loud sigh to draw his attention, I raise my eyebrows "Well? Anything?" The officer looks through me and doesn't answer.

In a few minutes the train comes to a halt. A man in a police uniform opens the door to the cabin. Apparently, the cops are here to meet the train. I'm transferred from the train security to the National Police of Marseille and whisked away in a police vehicle. At no time does anyone say anything to me or mention James' condition. When we arrive at the station house, I'm surrounded by uniformed police. I'm taken to the lockup and placed into a private cell. The door slamming behind me has a resonance I'm sure will mean my doom.

As I sit on the built-in cot, I roll my shoulders and try to alleviate some of the stiffness. I've been handcuffed for hours and my arms and hands are numb. I wonder how much longer I'll be left here.

*****

It's hours before there's a commotion outside the door. No one has checked on me and I have to use the bathroom. With a screech and a clang my cell opens and a man stands in the doorway backlit by the hallway light. I have an instant surge of panic and although I'm handcuffed and exhausted, I stand to face this new threat.

When the man comes into the room, I breathe a sigh of relief and sit. Detective Bernard rushes toward me and takes my arm to help me sit on the cot.

"Someone get me a clipper to get these ties off her!"

With a flurry of activity Detective Bernard releases my cuffs. Gently, he helps me move my arms. He sits next to me and massages them to help bring the circulation back. I smile at him in welcome and thankfulness, and ask, "Is he dead? Do you know? Is James dead?"

"*Oui*, my dear," he says, his warm, soft eyes look at me. "He is quite dead."

With a sigh of relief I hang my head and start to weep. I've been wound so tightly for so many hours the release of tension is overwhelming. The detective allows me to cry. He stands and ushers the men from my cell. "Give the girl some privacy now," he says as he shoos them out, all but one. When he comes back to sit with me, he pats my hand and says things like "shush now," and "it'll be all right." Detective Bernard reaches into his inside pocket to extract a monogrammed handkerchief and hands it to me.

As I quiet, the other man steps forward, he is dressed in a suit. Detective Bernard introduces him. "Ellen, this is Max Schwartzberg from the American Embassy. He's here to help and make certain your rights are upheld." I tenderly extend my arm to shake his hand.

"Ms. Thompson," he begins. "I'm sorely upset about the ordeal you've been through. We want you to have an examination at a medical facility post haste. I understand the security forces and the French police have protocol and they needed to hold you secure until their arrival in Marseille, but this was clearly a self-defense occurrence. Everyone we've spoken to, from the bystanders on the train to the security personnel who were present, have confirmed Detective Russell was in a murderous state."

"Murderous State," I mutter. "That may be the understatement of the year. Can you tell me if I'll be held in jail? Am I in trouble, legally?"

Mr. Schwartzberg moves to sit on my other side and takes off his glasses. He fishes a handkerchief from his pocket and begins to clean them. "In France, self-defense is very cut and dried. There are three criteria: time frame, danger and your reaction must be proportionate. From what I've heard, you fulfill all the criteria. You'll walk out this door in a matter of moments, on my honor and word."

I wipe my eyes and nose and have to smile. Mr. Schwartzberg is a funny little man and I like him already. If what he says is true, he'll be my new favorite person.

*****

Mr. Max Schwartzberg proves to be a legal genius and is perfectly correct in his estimations of my predicament. Very quickly, I'm released from the custody of the National Police and am to be whisked away to a hotel.

"No, Adrien. You're not understanding me." I stare intently at him while I once again state my position. "I'm not going anywhere. I need to see James' body. I need to see with my own eyes that he's dead."

It's a living nightmare I can't shake that he's somehow still alive. When I shut my eyes, all I see is his face. His face with the mask gone and the heinous smile as he leapt down the train aisle. They ask me to wait, to go to the hotel and get a hot shower, clean clothes and a meal, but I won't hear of it. How am I supposed to be by myself, let alone naked in a shower without absolute knowledge he's dead?

Finally, they realize I won't be dissuaded and agree to take me to the morgue. I look like a horror movie reject. I'm still in my clothing from the train. Once Detective Bernard arrived, I'd been allowed to wash my hands but I still have blood stains down my front. I look scary and smell of dried blood. I don't care. I will verify with my own eyes he's gone, that he won't turn up on my doorstep. It's hard enough to deal with what he'd hidden. I can't continue to fixate on the thought of his return.

As Detective Bernard brings the car, Mr. Schwartzberg walks me out of the police station. He opens the back door and I slide in and fasten my belt. Soon we head toward the morgue.

"I phoned ahead," says Detective Bernard, "so they know we're coming. There shouldn't be any problems."

"Thank you, Adrien," I say quietly from the back seat. "I hope you understand why I need to do this."

At Detective Bernard's nod, we fall silent for the trip downtown.

At the morgue, a technician meets, greets and leads us into a room. It's institutional and has stainless steel cabinets with many drawers. The temperature in the room is cold and it's terribly quiet. *Just like you see on TV*, I think. There's a peculiar scent in the air I can't identify. It smells like antiseptic and cold and I'm afraid to analyze it too closely for fear it'll be the smell of the dead. The technician leads us across the room, double checks a clipboard and opens one of the drawers. All his actions echo in the room and lend a surreal quality to this experience. As he pulls out the sliding bottom of the drawer, I suck in a deep breath. Detective Bernard steps to my side and places a hand on my shoulder. With a slight jump, I look from the shrouded body to the detective. "Are you ready, Ellen?" he asks gently.

I stare at the covered body with trepidation. Taking another deep breath I say, "Yes, let's get this over with."

Adrien nods to the technician and steps slightly closer. The technician folds the sheet back to reveal James' upper body.

He looks so pale, I think. Gingerly, I place my fingertips on his cheek. The coolness and stiffness of his skin registers and I jerk back quickly to rub my fingers on my palm in an effort to erase the memory. My eyes are drawn to the mangled mess of his throat. I hear my breathing and try to calm myself as panic fills me. "I need out of this room," I say and look at Detective Bernard. By his worried expression I can tell I must look a fright. He takes my arm and draws me into the hallway. I'm shivering. Chilled from the room and what it contains.

"Are you ready to go now, Ellen?" Adrien asks. "You need to take care of yourself. You need to get cleaned up and have something to eat."

With my head hanging, a small smile curves my lips and I pat his hand on my arm. "I'm ready. Thank you for this, Adrien. It's something I needed to do, to see. Now, maybe, I'll be able to sleep."

"We'll get you situated for your return to America as soon as possible," Mr. Schwartzberg says.

I jerk my head toward him with a look of surprise. "Oh no, Mr. Schwartzberg. I'm not returning to America, at least not right away. I need to meet with Mr. Monticelli."

The men look at each other and back at me in surprise. *Really? Do they think I am going to come all this way and go through all this and then run home when it's almost finished?*

With a weary shake of his head Detective Bernard steers me toward the door and says, "I may be able to help you with that."

22

I relax into the seat of the car Mr. Monticelli sent. It's a beautiful sedan with a professional, well-attired driver. I touch the seat and inhale the comforting smell of leather. It's nice of him to send a car and I'm certain Adrien Bernard had something to do with it. He's taken me under his wing and is already becoming something of a second father figure.

When we pull in front of the Monticelli estate, I'm mesmerized. The house and grounds sit on the coast and the south of France is stunning, almost painfully beautiful. The driver opens the back door and waits for me to exit the vehicle. He seems inclined to wait all day. I need to finish this, even if I learn nothing, so I take a deep breath and step out. With an urge to delay the moment, I walk to the cliff's edge and look at the Mediterranean Sea. The day is beautiful. The sun warm on my face. A small breeze blows inland off the water. It ruffles my skirt and hair as a chorus of sea birds call to one another and dive over a sea of turquoise.

Reluctantly, I turn from the view and giving the driver a small smile, I walk to the house. Although, house might be too common a word to describe the building. *Mansion*, I think. *Yep, mansion's a better word*. At the door, as I lift my hand to knock, it's opened by a man in a tailored suit. He's of small stature and appears very business-like and proper. With an inclination of his head he asks, "Ms.

Thompson?"

"Yes, I'm Ellen Thompson."

"Please come inside. Mr. Monticelli is expecting you. I'm Mathis, Mr. Monticelli's personal secretary." With a quiet snick the door closes and he leads me into the building. The hallway is grand, with artwork on the walls and beautiful sculptures displayed on tables. Unopened doors lead off the hallway at regular intervals. It's quiet, but comforting — like a museum.

"Is this a private collection?" I ask, with an indication to the works of art.

"Oh yes, Ma'am. This collection is indeed private. However, there's an extensive display of Adolphe Monticelli's work at the *Foundation Monticelli* in L'Estaque." I nod in understanding, though I don't know where that is.

Mathis leads me to a closed door. He knocks lightly, opens the door and steps aside for me to enter. With a polite smile and incline of my head I move into what appears to be an office, an office of an important man. I scan the room and notice more artwork tastefully displayed. A mahogany desk sits in front of a large window that overlooks manicured grounds and rising from the desk is a well-appointed middle-aged man. He's dressed in a suit, has grey hair and is about my height. He's attractive and obviously wealthy.

"Ms. Thompson," he says and approaches me with an extension of his hand. "Welcome to my home. As I told Detective Bernard, I don't usually conduct business from home but he was most persuasive on your behalf."

I give a quick smile. "Yes, I appreciate your time. Detective Bernard and I have become close in the past few weeks. He's an honorable man and I owe him a great deal."

With a nod, Mr. Monticelli motions to a set of wingback chairs along one wall. "Would you like to have a seat and we can discuss what he felt so strongly I would want to know?"

I sit and take a deep breath preparing to speak. At just that moment, Mathis returns with a cart of coffee. "Would you like *un café, Mademoiselle*?" he asks.

I relax even more. With a nod I say. "Oh yes, thank you. I do adore French coffee."

Once the coffee is served, Mathis closes the door quietly on his way out. Sipping my café, I'm happy for its warmth. I feel chilled and apprehensive with the knowledge the time has come to see if this trip will end here. *Has everything that happened been worth it?*

"Mr. Monticelli," I begin. "What can you tell me about your family's history with Van Gogh's painting "Poppy Flowers?"

With a furrowed brow and a question in his eyes, Arnaude Monticelli proceeds to tell me of his great grandfather's relationship with Vincent Van Gogh. He explains Van Gogh's interest in Adolphe's use of colors.

"I understand his use of colors was inspiration for Van Gogh to create the painting "Poppy Flowers." I confirm with a tilt of my head.

"Yes, this is true." He looks closely at me for a moment. "Ms. Thompson, what does this have to do with your visit?"

"I won't take up much of your time, Mr. Monticelli, but if you have a moment, I'd like to tell you a story..."

✶✶✶✶✶

When I run out of words, I lean back, relieved and exhausted and sip my now-cooled coffee. During the telling, Mr. Monticelli sat and listened, not interrupting. Now, he sits quietly, seemingly in deep thought.

"Ms. Thompson, that's a very interesting tale you weave." He looks at me intently. "Do you have the pieces, the clues, as you call them?"

I reach for my purse and pull out an envelope that contains the photos, notes and other articles. As I hand the envelope to Mr. Monticelli my breath catches with a flashback of handing an envelope to James. I breathe deeply to control a burst of panic and sadness. I remember that day in my hotel room. I was thrilled with the excitement and promise of the mystery surrounding "Poppy Flowers" and the excitement of a budding relationship. Then came the following days with their panic and betrayal. I catch Mr. Monticelli's eye as he watches me. I give him a small smile and he opens the envelope to withdraw the items. After studying each piece, he sets them on his lap and gazes at me with speculation.

"This is most interesting, Ms. Thompson. So you are proposing the two Italians who were stopped and questioned are this Maria and Angelo?"

"Yes, Sir," I answer. "I do believe that to be true and because Maria Cabana showed up in Paris in an attempt to reclaim the painting, I believe this proves Angelo stole it and left her when his obsession became too much, just as the note states. She had knowledge of the painting and of these items."

"You're curious if this Angelo came to see me?"

"Yes, Sir. We... I believe he's dying and his next stop is Marseille. Have you heard from him?"

With a small shake of his head he admits, "I'm sorry, Ms. Thompson. I have no knowledge of this man you seek. The other items, you purchased from an American man?" I didn't blame him for his confusion and the skepticism in his tone. This story is complex.

"No, Sir. I purchased a mirror from an Italian man in America. In the mirror I discovered the original note. When I went to speak with him I found him dead, murdered, in fact, and consequently found the music box which led to the other things."

"Cabana is a name I'm familiar with. They're an Italian family that's best described as a rival. A rival who has long pursued an unnatural interest in both my great grandfather and Van Gogh's painting "Poppy Flowers." Joseph Cabana, Sr., who died recently, had the misbegotten idea he was a decedent of my family and our legacy was his. He attempted to purchase and possibly steal many items over the years, though we have no proof. What was the name of this man in America from whom you purchased the mirror?"

"I only knew him as Bell, but after his murder I found out his first name was Joe." At my words Mr. Monticelli sits up straight in his chair and a look of surprise comes to his face. "What?" I ask. "Did I say something?"

"You see, Ms. Thompson, in Italian, Cabana means Bell." I let this information settle in my mind. "A few years ago, Joseph Cabana, Jr. disappeared and hasn't been heard from. I believe we can assume he went to America, for reasons we may never know."

Though this information answers some of the mystery behind Joe Bell, I'm still unable to resolve the fact I have no way to move forward with my search. It appears my quest will end in Marseille.

Mr. Monticelli takes a last look at the photo, notes and papyrus paper and returns them to me. "So, Ms. Thompson, how do you find Marseille?"

I answer truthfully, "I believe it's the most beautiful place I've ever seen. The sea is wonderful."

"And what do you do for your livelihood?"

"I work at the Detroit Institute of Art in America. I've loved items of art since as far back as I can remember." His interest and quiet way fills me with a sense of relaxation and I volunteer personal information. "As a child I went to the museums often with my parents. Working with art is all I've ever wanted to do."

"This may seem to be a proposition made with haste, but I don't often come across a person who has the ability to reason so decisively and who has such a love of art to come across the world; also, Adrien Bernard vouches for you." He hesitates and looks me over as he continues, "but we're looking for an assistant curator at the *Musée Monticelli.* It's a small museum named after my great grandfather and has many of his works. I'm curious if you may be interested in the position."

My mind blanks for an instant. This is the last thing I imagined would come of this day. "Really?" is all I can say.

With a smile at my dumfounded look, Arnaude Monticelli nods. "Yes, Ms. Thompson. Really."

"Wow!" I don't know what else to say. "May I take a moment to think it over and get my bearings?" Laughing I add, "I certainly didn't expect this from our visit."

"Of course, please take your time. You can give your information to Mathis and he'll e-mail you the particulars." As he stands, I stand with him. "I'm sorry to end our conversation, but I should return to my work."

Mr. Monticelli and I walk down the hallway toward the exit. He tells me about the effort his family continues to make for the preservation of artworks — not just his grandfather's.

A swinging door to our left opens and Mathis steps out.

"*Pardon Moi,* Mr. Monticelli and *Mademoiselle* Thompson," he says with an incline of his head. "You have a phone call that cannot wait, sir."

Mr. Monticelli nods to his secretary. He turns to me and says, "Mathis will see you to the exit. I hope to hear from you soon. Safe travels, Ms. Thompson."

"Thank you for your time, Mr. Monticelli. It was a pleasure to meet you and I'll definitely get back with you about the job opportunity."

As I walk down the entryway from the estate I look over the Mediterranean Sea. With a half turn, I glance back at the building. All through my interview with Mr. Monticelli I had a low grade vibration going on. Problem is, I don't know why or what. Sometimes I wish my Buzz could speak English and tell me what it wants.

With a twist I face the sea. The sun shines and sea birds call. I take a deep breath and think how much has changed in just a few weeks. Can I let go of my quest to find "Poppy Flowers?" Where will I even go from here? The clues have run out. Should I take this opportunity that has presented itself? Can I return to my life in Michigan? I'm a different person than the woman who purchased the mirror from Joe Bell.

I approach the cliff face where the waves crash. *What a wonderful, relaxing sound,* I think as I continue to stare to the horizon. I unzip a pocket on my bag and remove the key I took from Joe Bell's hand. I wonder, *what's it for? Why's it important enough he held it even in death?* I may never know the answers to all of my questions. I unclasp the chain and medallion from my neck. Carefully, I slide the key onto my chain and replace it around my neck. I look at the two for a moment and then tuck them into the front of my dress. As I turn back toward the waiting car, a sea bird swoops near me. It catches my eye. I watch it dive and hover on the winds, wishing I could be as free. I slide into the car still watching the bird.

✶✶✶✶✶

So that's my story. Thinking back, even though I'm the one who lived it, it feels like a dream.

Do you believe me? Do I believe me?

Who am I now? Where do I go?

Who are the "Poppy Flowers" calling to…

23

Epilogue

MONTICELLI

TWO YEARS AGO

Arnaude Monticelli looks from the work on his desk to see his butler standing in the doorway.

"Yes?" he queries the man.

"There's a man asking to see you. He's ill kept and I would send him away, but he says he has a piece of artwork you'll be interested in."

"Send him in." Mr. Monticelli pushes from his desk with a furrow on his brow.

When the man comes into his office, Mr. Monticelli stands. His butler is correct, the man is ill-kept and smells as though he quit bathing ages ago. He looks half crazed. His clothing is dirty and tattered.

"What can I help you with?" Mr. Monticelli asks.

"Mr. Monticelli…." The man begins. "I can no longer live with my sin. You must take it and I will be forgiven." The man reaches into his coat and withdraws a rolled up canvas. As he steps forward to take the canvas, Mr. Monticelli looks down at it. Quizzically, he looks back at the man. He notices in the other hand, the man holds a gun.

"Wait, no, please, don't..." Mr. Monticelli puts up his hands in a warding gesture. Before he can finish his thought, the man raises the gun to his own head and pulls the trigger.

✶✶✶✶✶

Shaking off the memory, Arnaude Monticelli watches Ellen Thompson from the upstairs window as she leaves. His secretary, Mathis stands behind him ready to assist with whatever is necessary. "You think I'm wrong to offer her a position at *Musée Monticelli?*"

"It's not for me to say, *Monsieur.*"

Arnaude Monticelli turns from the window. His attention is caught by the painting which hangs behind his secretary. It's small, but compelling. It may be dangerous to have her so close. They will see...

The End

ABOUT THE AUTHOR

Vicki B. Williamson lives in Montana with her husband, Mark and their Golden Retriever, Ripley.

Finding Poppies is her first novel.

Sign up to receive the lasted book release updates, as well as information about contest and giveaways at Contact Information:
https://vickibwilliamsonauthor.wordpress.com/